Maia didn't know how to answer Niko.

It wasn't that she'd feared a pregnancy might be unsafe—she'd feared she might not get pregnant at all, what with how irregular everything was. Yet now she was apparently pregnant and she hadn't slept with anyone!

Niko waited, clearly wanting something from her, but she didn't know what it was. His gaze on her intensified. "I would like you to have this baby, Maia."

The thought that she wouldn't hadn't even occurred to her. That reply came instantly to her lips. But she bit it back. She needed to understand more. While what he'd just said *sounded* conciliatory—a *request* not an order— she suspected that was somewhat foreign to him. Sweat slid down her spine. She was pregnant with a king's baby. What would he want from her? How did he see this moving? She needed to ascertain how far he would take his control and power over her. So she gestured around the room's palatial splendor. "Do I really have a choice?"

Innocent Royal Runaways

Royally bound...to a king!

Kings Niko and Luc are best friends and brothers in honor. They are two very different leaders who rule two very different kingdoms. One lives in the cool mountains of Europe, one in the hot heart of the Pacific. But they are both united by their dedication to duty and their people.

Only neither have factored desire into the equation... And that's exactly what Maia and Zara bring to their lives. Desire so intense that, even when they try, it's impossible to outrun and impossible to hide!

Read Niko and Maia's story in
Impossible Heir for the King
Available now!

And discover Luc and Zara's story
Return of the Long-Lost King
Coming soon!

Natalie Anderson

IMPOSSIBLE HEIR FOR THE KING

HARLEQUIN®
PRESENTS™

ISBN-13: 978-1-335-59272-9

Impossible Heir for the King

Copyright © 2023 by Natalie Anderson

For questions and comments about the quality of this book, please contact us at CustomerService@Harlequin.com.

Harlequin Enterprises ULC
22 Adelaide St. West, 41st Floor
Toronto, Ontario M5H 4E3, Canada
www.Harlequin.com

Printed in U.S.A.

USA TODAY bestselling author **Natalie Anderson** writes emotional contemporary romance full of sparkling banter, sizzling heat and uplifting endings—perfect for readers who love to escape with empowered heroines and arrogant alphas who are too sexy for their own good. When she's not writing, you'll find Natalie wrangling her four children, three cats, two goldfish and one dog... and snuggled in a heap on the sofa with her husband at the end of the day. Follow her at natalie-anderson.com.

Books by Natalie Anderson

Harlequin Presents

The Night the King Claimed Her
The Boss's Stolen Bride

Billion-Dollar Christmas Confessions

Carrying Her Boss's Christmas Baby

Rebels, Brothers, Billionaires

Stranded for One Scandalous Week
Nine Months to Claim Her

Jet-Set Billionaires

Revealing Her Nine-Month Secret

The Christmas Princess Swap

The Queen's Impossible Boss

Visit the Author Profile page
at Harlequin.com for more titles.

For the incomparable Louise—we might have polar-opposite processes but what giggles, support and inspiration we do share! I cannot thank you enough. Here's to all the joy.

PROLOGUE

'How was it possible for such a mistake to be made?' Niko Ture, King of the North Pacific nation of Piri-nu, stared at his most trusted soldier waiting for an explanation he knew could never be satisfactory. 'The level of incompetence is beyond comprehension.'

'Agreed,' Captain Pax Williams answered.

Niko—far more emotional—reeled as a raft of possible appalling consequences struck him. 'Was it an accident or was this deliberate?'

'The investigation is underway. I only found out through a security contact at the clinic who spotted the anomaly.' Pax bent his head. 'But—'

'We need to bring that woman here now,' Niko interrupted sharply. 'I need to know. Where is she? *Who* is she?'

Wordlessly his captain handed him a slim file. Irritated, Niko flicked it open and skimmed the sparse text, frowning at the highlighted points.

'I've tracked the vessel she's aboard,' Pax said. 'With your permission I'll lead an extraction team at 0400. We'll have her at the palace before dawn.'

Niko stared at the photo of the young woman, still

thunderstruck at the information he'd just learned. Nondescript, frankly dull-looking in those loose black clothes, he ordinarily wouldn't give her a second glance. But this was no ordinary situation. Apparently—*impossibly*—this plain woman might be the mother of his unborn baby. 'I'm going with you.'

He knew Pax was about to argue and he lifted his head and stopped him with a look. 'I'm boarding that boat. You would too, if you were me.'

Pax stared back for a split second before inclining his head. 'Of course, sir.'

Niko looked again at the face of the young woman who was somehow caught up in a palace intrigue of epic proportions. Was she innocent or was she guilty?

There was only one way to find out.

CHAPTER ONE

MAIA FLYNN FASTENED the scarf holding her hair out of the way and sighed at the bane of her life. The coffee machine's regular temperamental performance issues were always worse when someone else had tried to use the thing. Late last night someone clearly had, given grounds were scattered over the galley. They'd left the resulting chaos for her to clean. Nothing new there except today that stale coffee smell was particularly nauseating. Yet it was a shame she didn't drink the stuff. She could do with a caffeine kick because even though she'd slept through the midnight coffee-making mess, once more she hadn't had enough sleep. She felt constantly tired from the pressure of too many guests, too much stress and no end in sight. She ought to be used to it, but in the last few weeks her baseline fatigue level had only worsened.

Ignoring her father's miserly 'not for the crew' rules, she poured a little glass of the premium pineapple juice reserved for their wealthy—invariably rude—guests. Then she pulled her favourite whittling knife from her pocket and the small wood block she'd been shaping in her limited spare seconds. She needed a moment of mindfulness before dealing with the destruction caused by the spilled coffee. But as she focused on the blade a muffled thud sounded from an upper deck. She paused warily. The guests shouldn't wake for a couple of hours yet, which meant it might be her father, the captain of this 'luxury' yacht. Though generally he didn't surface this early either. Holding her breath, she listened intently but after a few seconds there was nothing more. She sipped some juice and turned back to the wood. This was her favourite part of the day—pre-dawn— when the sky gently lightened before the slow emergence of the sun. It mattered little that she could see it only from the small porthole in the galley. It was the only time she had to herself, it was peaceful and she always felt a hit of optimism—*today might be different*.

In reality she knew she faced a relentlessly long day prepping food for the guests and the crew. She rarely left the boat that had been her home her entire life and while she yearned to escape, it wasn't possible yet. Not when she had nowhere else to go, no money to get there with and no formal qualifications to 'prove' her skills and get another job. It wasn't like her bully of a father would ever give her a reference. He'd be too furious that she'd dared walk out. But she needed to find a solution soon both for her independence and her health. She wished she'd been able to consult the doctor when they were last on shore but her father had phoned in the middle of her appointment and she'd had to leave before getting the results of the few tests they'd been able to complete—

There it was again. Another sound out of place, so soft she almost didn't notice it. But a sixth sense struck, shooting sensation down her spine. She whirled to face the doorway, knocking the glass of juice as she did. She suspected it might be a still-drunk guest from last night coming for something to eat.

It wasn't.

For a split second she stared at him—stunned and ignoring the smash of the glass and splash of the juice at her feet. Tall, lean, clad entirely in black—from the close-fitting skullcap to the mask covering his mouth— he even had some kind of stuff smudged on his skin to obscure what little of his face remained visible. Horror hit. He looked like a mercenary. But for an infinite second his brown eyes bored into hers—as rich as the coffee grounds, only far warmer. They locked on her and a lightning strike of *something* hit.

She couldn't speak. Couldn't scream. Then she remembered what she held and lifted her knife, amazed her hand wasn't shaking.

'Don't. Don't be scared,' he whispered, holding his hands wide in surrender. He didn't move a step nearer. 'It's okay.'

It wasn't *okay*. But she froze, trying to understand why he was here, why he was hesitant—why he almost looked *worried*. Maia lifted her chin and pretended her little knife was so much more than it was. She'd get to her cabin. She'd lock the door and hide. They could take whatever they wanted then. For a second she even felt she had a chance because he, despite his size, seemed so oddly wary.

She stepped backwards. He still didn't move but his gaze was intent upon her. Emboldened, she moved faster but the spilled juice proved treacherous. Her foot slid out from beneath her and despite her sudden lurch she couldn't recover. She whacked her wrist on the bench as she flung out her arms to stop her fall. The knife clattered as it hit the floor. But *she* didn't. Because in the swiftest move she'd ever seen a man make he caught her.

'Easy, *easy*. I've got you.' He lifted her effortlessly. Lifted her close. So close.

She grabbed hold of him—tightly—instinctively relieved she'd not fallen. Instinctively reaching for *strength*. His hands gently, swiftly moved over her back, both pressing her into his chest and checking she was still all in one piece. It was oddly—*crazily*—comforting.

'Okay?' he muttered.

She could smell the sea, mixed with something spiced—something her senses decided was *interesting*. She closed her eyes and tried not to breathe—not to notice the appalling, raw appeal of him as he pulled her more tightly against him. This was the closest she'd been to another human being in a very long time and it was freaking her out in all *kinds* of ways. Struggling to process what was happening, she froze when she heard a low murmur from behind her and then felt an answering vibration in his chest. He was talking to someone else and she was too stunned to even understand the words. But she understood that there was more than one of them. Which meant this was a raid. Probably for the cash they suspected they carried on board. The perils of a gambling cruise alone in the northern Pacific Ocean. Her father had a gun and wasn't afraid to use it, but somehow they'd snuck aboard unseen. Which meant they had *skills*.

Panic finally fired adrenalin through her. She had to fight for her life. She wriggled and managed to lift her head and stare up into his eyes.

'No,' she muttered and drew breath to scream.

But he was swift again. He clamped his hand over her mouth. She twisted her chin and locked her teeth on the flesh she found. She bit. Hard.

He flinched but didn't release her. He merely pulled her back into his body.

'Please, don't,' that deep voice roughly whispered into her ear. 'I'm not here to hurt you, Maia. I'm so sorry, but there's no choice. We're leaving. Now.'

He knew her name?

She was so shocked that her body slackened—releasing her jaw she collapsed against him so completely that he had to widen his stance to stop them stumbling. Now both his arms were around her again and it felt so shockingly secure that she didn't even think to scream. She sensed rapid movement around her. In seconds someone from behind her taped something over her mouth and dropped a dark cloth over her head, blackening everything while the first man still held her. She felt him draw a deep breath and mentally willed herself to become a dead weight that would be impossible to lift. Only he hoisted her in his arms like she weighed little more than a small seashell. He didn't toss her over his shoulder in the classic firefighters hold but cradled her against his chest—as if she were something delicate and precious. It should be cumbersome yet they were moving. Fast. Up the stairs and outside—she felt the lightest breeze before they moved down again almost immediately. They were leaving the boat. He held her tighter still as the world lurched and heaven help her, she curled frightened fingers into his top and burrowed her head against him, seeking the stability she sensed within him.

After what felt like an age of chaotic movement, he finally sat while still cocooning her in his arms. He rested one arm heavily over her legs while the other was a steel band clamping her against his chest. In the silence she heard his heartbeat steadying and his calm, determined breathing. He was measuring his own response. Suddenly she felt oddly *safe*.

She'd lost it mentally, surely. She had her mouth covered and was blindfolded. She had no idea who he was or where he was taking her. To have Stockholm syndrome in less than twenty seconds had to be some kind of record. Just because he smelt good and had meltingly deep brown eyes, solid, warm muscles and had offered an apologetic whisper... Her suddenly sensual response was dreadfully inappropriate. She forced herself to focus beyond her personal sensations.

She heard the quiet splashes of an oar in the water. Yes, there was definitely more than one of them and she was definitely in danger. She shivered, shrinking inwardly.

His arms tightened fractionally. 'I promise I'm not going to hurt you, Maia.'

That really was a hint of regret in that rough whisper.

Who was he? She didn't recognise his voice. She didn't think he was ex-crew or a previous guest. What did he want with her?

This had been perfectly planned and executed. But why? She didn't think anyone much knew who she even was. So, either there'd been some kind of mistake or she'd been cased as an easy target for trafficking. Yet that wasn't an issue in these parts. Maybe she was to be the first.

Sure, she already was a slave of a sort for her father but she wasn't in physical danger with him—that threat was more emotional. But *this* man? She grew even more hyper-aware of his hard-packed muscles and the all-encapsulating size of him and that faint scent sea-spray and mouth-watering spice. That sensuality resurged. She shrank further in on herself to try to stop it. And all that resulted from her doing that was that he held her closer still as if he were wordlessly wrapping comfort around her. And then he offered the words too—as if he could read her mind.

'You're safe,' he said huskily. 'I promise you're safe.'

She didn't know how long it was before he lifted her too easily again. She was only a few inches shy of six feet—taller than many men so this was a weird feeling of weightlessness and a complete loss of control. There was only a moment of rocking, uncertain movement before he sat again, keeping her locked in his arms the entire time. She heard an engine roar to life and knew she was now aboard a bigger boat. Sure enough, she could feel the hull of the speedboat smacking against the water as it raced forwards. Wind penetrated the hood on her head. The man who held her remained utterly silent this time.

Then whispers. Orders. Movement around her. She

was carried again—heard not just his footsteps but several people's. Car doors. Motion at speed. Still silence.

She briefly felt the sun on her arms before it went cold. Then they'd entered a building. Maia was exhausted but he'd held her all this time—surely he must be exhausted too? Then she heard only his footsteps. He set her down on something soft and finally released her. She stiffened—stupidly scared by losing the reassurance of his embrace. What was going to happen now?

'Wait here, Maia.'

His footsteps receded. A door closed.

Her hands were free but Maia remained frozen, desperately listening to determine if she was truly alone. At last, she lifted the hood from her head and blinked rapidly, adjusting her eyes to the bright light of day. She winced as she peeled the tape from her mouth and then stared, shocked. This was no grimy basement. There were no chains or ropes or anything of nightmarish horror awaiting her. This room was resplendent. She wasn't on a bed but a plush sofa and other sumptuous lounge seats faced her. Was this some fancy hotel?

I'm not going to hurt you, Maia.

That rough promise rang in her ears but she'd been afraid to believe it. But this room threw her off balance. Ornate wooden carvings decorated the doorways—she knew the skill with which they'd been carved and while the furniture she sat on was modern and comfortable, there were antiques in the corners and art on the walls that weren't hotel standard. They were national gallery–worthy. A film of sweat slicked across her skin. She was so far out of her league. There were three doors she could try but she figured they were probably locked or guarded or both. She edged towards the wide window to see what she could from there instead.

Maia was used to pristine views of Pacific beauty. It was the clues on the land that made her jaw drop and there was one very big clue right in the middle of the immaculate gardens below her. A tall pole with the flag of Piri-nu barely fluttering in the still warmth.

The wealthy nation was situated in the Pacific Ocean between Hawai'i and Marquesas. They were the islands Maia would most likely call home although she really considered herself to be stateless—she wasn't sure she even had a birth certificate. But her father liked to work near Piri-nu because of the extreme wealth of its visitors. The nation was prosperous not just from agriculture, nor tourism because of its natural beauty, but also as an aerospace technology hub. One of the world's largest telescopes was situated here together with a massive space rocket launch infrastructure that attracted billionaires and geniuses from around the world.

Any remaining fear faded in the face of pure confusion. This was laughable. Why would anyone want to kidnap *her* and bring her to the palace of the playboy king?

CHAPTER TWO

MAIA HEARD VOICES at one of the doors and backed against the window to keep as far as possible from whoever was about to walk in. Her pulse lifted as the door opened. Would it be her captor with the muscles and salty-spice scent?

The man who walked in was powerful, self-assured, stunning. Her hard-pumping heart made blood pound in her ears. He was as tall. He was as strong. But this was the king—Niko Ture himself!

As he closed the door she couldn't stop herself staring, snared in the deep, dark, coffee-coloured eyes that gleamed like the water at sunset. Even though she didn't have a smart phone she'd seen his image often enough on the old television in the crew room where they sometimes watched the news so she recognised those sculpted features now—the angular jaw, the distinctive high cheekbones. The stunning symmetry of his bone structure almost made her swallow her tongue. But she'd not been able to see the jaw of her kidnapper because of that mask. So she studied this man more intently—unable to quite believe the direction of her thoughts. He kept one hand in his trouser pocket, giving him a louche look, and that snow-white shirt was a touch too perfect, lovingly skimming that lean muscled chest. He didn't usually look this serious on that screen. He was usually smiling.

'Maia,' he said. 'I'm Niko, King of Piri-nu.'

'I'm aware,' she gritted.

Was she supposed to curtsey? Because that wasn't going to happen. Every muscle had gone into shock and she couldn't actually move a millimetre. The impossibly handsome, popular royal was her total opposite. Had *he* summoned her to be brought before him? Surely not. How would he have even *heard* of her? Her poor heart pumped even harder.

'You may call me Niko.'

Why would she call him by his first name? There was no reason for her to have that privilege.

He casually strolled closer with the assured, panther-like grace of a man well used to the effect he had on ordinary people. Especially women. And yes, that included her.

'I apologise for your unexpected journey,' he added smoothly. 'I understand it was a little rough.'

He 'understood'? As he neared she could only stare like a stunned fool at his beauty. His face gleamed with vitality. Well, except for *one* patch of his skin just above his jaw which seemed slightly muddied. Maia blinked as her suspicions—now confirmed—stalled her breath. She breathed a little deeper and caught the slight scent—

The *arrogance*!

Her brain fuzzed. He *was* the one who'd pressed her so tightly to his body! He was the one who'd whispered those reassurances in her ear. He was the one who'd carried her so easily. But suddenly his looks didn't have the same 'stunned mullet' effect on her. Sure, she was growing hotter by the second but now it was anger, not latent lust. Did he think he could get away with anything if he suavely offered some minimal, meaningless apology?

Probably. No doubt he'd been doing it his whole life—doing whatever he wanted. But right now he was *lying* to her because he knew exactly how *unexpected* her journey had been. Exactly how rough. Because he'd been right there all along.

'You've not quite cleaned all your war paint off.' She bristled, pointing to a spot on her cheek, mirroring where the smear of black was still stuck on him.

His gaze sharpened and his mouth twitched as he leisurely lifted his hand and rubbed the mark away.

But Maia glared pointedly at the hand he'd kept in his pocket all this time. 'Did I break your skin with my bite or merely leave a bruise?'

'Did you know it was me all along or only just work it out now?' That smile broadened to genuine amusement. He wasn't at all ashamed that she'd caught him out.

Maia was stunned into stillness all over again. She shouldn't feel anything but outrage but her body decided to do its own thing. Her breasts tightened and her breathing shortened and she was shocked to realise the tension she now felt was fully sensual in nature. She obviously hadn't been around any attractive men recently, so her body had decided to flare up in front of the first one she saw. But it was unacceptable. This entire situation was unacceptable.

'It seems you need to practice your abduction skills,' she snapped.

'Perhaps I do.' He gave another flash of that unrepentant smile.

But this king had no need to abduct anyone. He was a wildly popular playboy who'd ascended to the throne five years ago after the death of his grandfather—the crown skipping a generation because of the tragic death of Niko's father when Niko was in his teens.

'Forgive me for being stunned that you've run out of suitable women to sleep with and must now resort to stealing perfect strangers from their homes in the middle of the night,' she said.

'I'll forgive you anything.' He lazily nodded. 'And you are indeed a perfect stranger. But the truth is I have no need to abduct women to sleep with me. That's not why you're here.'

Of course it wasn't.

Humiliation slithered from the cesspit of queasiness roiling in her lower belly and spread across her skin in a heated blaze. He probably wanted her to be a maid—to make his coffee and fresh pastry and bring it to him and his lover-of-the-day in bed.

But that didn't explain why'd he brought her here under the cover of darkness. Why he'd not just asked her, nor told anyone else on the boat his intentions. But maybe he'd ensured no one had seen her journey and her arrival at the palace because she wasn't *worthy* to be seen here. She glanced down, deeply aware of her dishevelment. Shame sloshed. She felt hot and clumsy and ugly in her worn galley clothing. She was nothing like the beautiful women Niko was always photographed with when he was abroad. And she was not Piri-nu society worthy.

She was the illegitimate child of a waitress and a gambler. Her mother had run off before Maia had turned four, unable to fight her father's controlling nature anymore. Unfortunately, she'd left with a man who'd turned out to be even more controlling and he'd not wanted another man's child. He'd made her mother cut contact with Maia completely. Most of the time Maia didn't think about it, but right now she was alone and afraid. And her father would never try to rescue her from this, he'd be far more likely to try to extract something for himself. Such as money.

So she would face this obvious mistake down and she would survive all by herself. She was good at that.

'Why *am* I here?' Maia pushed through the mortification and asked.

His smile had faded and his razor-like cheekbones made him look starkly sombre. 'Because I'm afraid you might be pregnant with my baby.'

She stared at him, nonplussed. 'You *what*?'

'I think you're pregnant. With my child.'

The man was mad. Certifiable. Maia laughed. Except it veered dangerously close to hysterics in a nanosecond. She gasped, biting the emotion back. She refused to fall apart in front of *anyone* and certainly not this entitled, arrogant piece of work.

'You know, it doesn't surprise me that you can't recall who you've slept with,' she said, masking fear with sarcastic fury. 'I understand there are multitudes of women who've had the dubious honour of being in your bed but *I* am not one of them and I never will be.'

'I'm aware that we haven't slept together.' He regarded her steadily, apparently unmoved by her snark about his hyperactive sex life. 'And I agree that such an event is extremely unlikely.'

She paused, cut by his quick, harsh reply. But of course it was true. He'd never want to sleep with her when he had his pick...

She glanced again at her black capri pants and plain T-shirt, work-stained and worn. Usually she didn't serve the clients. Her father preferred his nubile stewards do that. Maia remained out of sight and she liked it that way—or at least in that particular environment she did. She plaited her hair, coiled it into a bun and secured a scarf over the top. It was hot in the galley and the last thing she wanted was a loose strand falling into her food. But she'd never felt as unattractive as she did this second. No make-up. No pretty nails. Her style was best summed up as brutal utilitarianism. By necessity, not choice. Her father didn't think she needed a clothing allowance and as she rarely left the boat she didn't need anything that was too delicate to work in.

King Niko was watching her intently. 'Eleven weeks ago you went to the Coral Shore Women's Clinic. You were a walk-in who benefitted from a last-minute cancellation.'

Maia watched seriousness mute the gleam of his brown eyes.

'You were there because you had some personal concerns but you didn't get the chance to talk through them with the doctor,' he said. 'Instead you had an initial physical examination with a nurse practitioner. Or you thought that's what was happening. A routine smear test of some sort.'

'How do you know this?' She was beyond humiliated that the king knew such private details about her.

'But after that physical, the clinician left the room and for some reason you didn't stay to see the doctor. You left, telling the receptionist you couldn't wait any longer. Your boat left port only a half hour later and you've not returned to land since.'

Her heart raced. 'I live on board my father's charter vessel. I'm part of the crew.'

'Is the rest of the crew unpaid as well?'

The earth rolled beneath her feet. How did he know *that*? *Why* did he know that? And how could he possibly think she might be *pregnant*?

She felt the walls closing in as he advanced upon her. Was that a flicker of regret in his eyes? If so, it was swiftly obliterated by steely determination and he didn't stop talking. He didn't stop saying this crazy stuff in that too clinical tone as he stepped too close for her comfort.

'What you didn't know was that there had been a miscommunication within the medical centre staff. The clinician who entered your room wasn't aware the other appointment had been cancelled. That appointment was for an insemination. You were wearing a mask and you are not dissimilar in appearance to the woman who'd been meant to be there.'

'Not dissimilar?' Maia's heart lodged in her throat. 'An insemination?' He couldn't possibly mean what…

He couldn't possibly be serious. 'Why would they have a sample of your...' She hesitated.

She might be inexperienced but she'd grown up surrounded by salty seafarers, many of whom called elements by their most base name possible. But not, perhaps, in front of a king.

'Traditionally a prince couldn't be proclaimed the immediate heir without first proving his virility,' he said. 'By providing the *next* heir. This was to preserve the lineage and keep the crown within the family. Usually this wasn't a problem as any heir was generally married and had procreated long before the elder king passed on. But I was pretty young when I became crown prince and had no intention of marrying and fathering a child at that point in my life. Fortunately I was able to prove my virility by more modern means.'

She was so appalled any decision to mind her mouth was forgotten. 'You mean they studied your spunk like you're a stallion or something?'

His eyebrows shot up. 'You're asking if they treated me literally like a stud? Then yes, that's exactly what happened.'

She was both appalled and fascinated. What a weird world the man lived in. 'But all of that must have been ages ago.'

She didn't know exactly when his father had died, only that it had been sudden. A second tragedy since his mother had died in an accident a couple of years before. 'Why would they have kept that sample?'

'Apparently, it was considered too precious and they wouldn't dream of just discarding it.'

'As if it was some sort of sacred artefact?' She gaped, her mind boggled.

He suddenly laughed. 'You disagree with that assessment?'

But this was no time to be laughing. And he 'discarded' it all the time, did he not? With all those stars and models and socialites that he seduced when he was overseas. 'You didn't know they'd kept it?'

As his smile faded Maia tried to understand the outrageous complexity of what he'd told her. An awful thought stuck her. Had he a partner that no one knew anything about? Was he trying for a child with someone who would be feeling so hurt and betrayed right now? Yet why would that be necessary—wouldn't they just try for a baby the usual way? Unless there were problems, which just made everything worse. And the man wasn't even engaged to anyone—or was he? And was she really having all kinds of *wrong* reactions to someone else's lover?

'How was it possible for such a mistake to be made?' She asked desperately, trying not to consider the implications of what he'd said.

'My question exactly.'

'*Why* would they have taken your sample? It's—'

'Being investigated and those found responsible will feel the consequences,' he interrupted stiffly. 'What has occurred is unforgivable. I can only apologise that you've been caught up in it.'

'But why had they decided to use it?' She frowned. 'Do you think it was deliberate?'

'That's not your concern. Rest assured there was only the one sample so this can never happen again, but we must deal with the situation before us now.' The stark expression in his eyes sent a shaft of foreboding through her. 'I brought you here to do a pregnancy test so we can be sure this error hasn't resulted in a more permanent complication,' he said grimly.

Maia didn't move. She was unable to believe that what she'd thought was a routine smear test had actually been a syringe full of the king's semen. And now she might… She might…

No. It was beyond mortifying that she'd not even *known* what that clinician had actually been doing. But it had been her first ever smear test and she'd not exactly been watching. She'd been so embarrassed to be exposed like that to someone she didn't know she'd stared the other way. She'd not asked the woman any questions because she'd been too shy. She'd been building up the courage to do that with the doctor. But when the woman had left the room Maia's father had called to demand she return to the boat immediately as they'd had an unexpected booking. He'd been furious she'd left in the first place. She'd fled—assuming she'd get notified of any abnormal results. But she certainly hadn't expected something like *this*.

'It's not possible,' she muttered. Surely she would know? But she hadn't known *anything*. She was more than naive, she was ignorant and never had it hurt more that her mother had abandoned her. She'd never had the sex talk. She'd never been told anything—she'd had to figure it out herself and frankly, her sporadic internet searches had been somewhat unreliable. 'There's no way I would have gotten pregnant from that…'

'It is very, very unlikely, but it *is* possible,' Niko

said. 'So we simply need to rule it out. Get that negative test and I'll ensure you're back on your boat within the hour.'

She went very still. 'But if it isn't negative…?'

There was a brief hesitation before he brought back that beautiful smile. 'If that happens, we'll work that out then. But it is unlikely.'

But Maia wasn't overly reassured because now she thought about the fatigue that had been bothering her the last few weeks. The stench of the coffee grounds. The irregularity of her monthly cycle was nothing new but what if…? And she'd thought the slight tightness of her trousers was from sampling too many of her pastries recently. Because she'd craved the croissants more and more. Just plain. And what about the unusual bout of seasickness she'd experienced only last week when she was more likely to get land-sick than seasick?

She felt terribly ill right now.

'I have a doctor waiting,' Niko added firmly. 'You simply need to provide a sample.'

She stared at him blankly.

'You'll understand that this is of the utmost concern. I am the *king*, Maia.'

She heard the edge as he underlined that word. His power. And he assumed she was his subject, didn't he? But she was Maia Flynn and she lived beyond the borders of anyone's world—half shadowed, not participating wholly anywhere. They skated into international waters while her father ran his not-quite-legal business dealings and high-stakes gambling cruises.

Maia had become skilled to secure her own safety— learning to cook from the grizzled French chef who'd been her best friend and better guardian to her than any other. But in doing so she'd cemented her own imprisonment because her father hadn't allowed her to leave the boat since. She created the things his clients liked for free. Chef Stefan had lost his job and she still felt guilty for being the reason when he'd only ever been kind to her.

'There's a restroom through that door,' Niko added crisply. 'Everything you need is in there.'

She had no choice to comply. And there was far more than she needed in the bathroom—it was full of unopened luxury toiletries that would delight even the most demanding guest. The lone medical sample container on the counter was incongruous. And terrifying. When she emerged a few minutes later an impassive man wearing a white coat was waiting for her. Awkwardly she gave him the container and he immediately fussed over a small side table where King Niko now stood.

The doctor turned to explain the process. 'Two lines will appear on a positive result—'

'Doctor, please leave us.' Niko abruptly dismissed him.

Maia turned. The beautiful man now looked every inch the ruthless mercenary who'd kidnapped her in the first place. His wild displeasure was menacing.

She darted a glance behind him and saw the white plastic stick on the table. Lines had already appeared in that little window. *Two* lines. Devastation barrelled into her. She was pregnant.

'It can't be right,' she mumbled hopelessly. 'It just *can't* be right.'

The doctor passed her and she thought she saw compassion briefly flicker in his face before he melted from the room.

'Amongst other things a DNA test will now have to be performed.'

She stared, all the more confused. '*Why?*'

'To ensure that the baby is mine, not some other man's.'

Her jaw dropped. For a long moment their gazes meshed. His eyes narrowed and she heard his sharp intake of breath. She made herself glance away, more humiliated than ever. She was horribly aware of heat scorching her whole body. There'd been no man. *Ever.* But some instinct warned her not to reveal that to him. She needed to act as if she had some sort of street cred. And she needed to scrape together some kind of control in this rapidly deteriorating situation.

'Of course,' she muttered belatedly. 'I will agree to that.'

Incredulity flared in his eyes at her reply. 'You will? I'm so glad.' He studied her for another moment. 'The doctor will do a full physical examination and talk with you. We need to ensure this is something you can safely manage.'

'Safely?'

'You should not suffer adversely because of this incident. Your health…'

She realised he had concerns because she'd gone to the doctor in the first place. 'It should be fine,' she mumbled, embarrassment burning her skin hotter still. 'It was just painful.'

'Sex?'

She gritted her teeth, her humiliation now total. 'No. My cycle. My periods. They're irregular and painful.'

'Oh, okay.' He frowned. 'Please be frank with the doctor. We will take every possible care of your health.'

Maia didn't know how to answer. It wasn't that she'd feared a pregnancy might be unsafe—she'd feared she might not get pregnant at all what with how irregular everything was. Yet now she was apparently pregnant and she hadn't slept with anyone!

He waited, clearly wanting something from her, but she didn't know what it was. His gaze on her intensified. 'I would like you to have this baby, Maia.'

The thought that she wouldn't hadn't even occurred to her. That reply came instantly to her lips. But she bit it back. She needed to understand more. While what he'd just said *sounded* conciliatory—a *request* not an order—she suspected that was somewhat foreign to him. Sweat slid down her spine. She was pregnant with a king's baby. What would he want from her? How did he see this moving? She needed to ascertain how far he would take his control and power over her. Because the *last* thing she wanted was for her life to be controlled by another man. She'd lived too long like that already. So she gestured around the room's palatial splendour. 'Do I really have a choice?'

His jaw tightened. 'If you don't wish to have a relationship with the child once they are born, that is your decision.'

The sweat slicked over her skin turned to ice in an instant. It was like she was suffering from the instant onset of a tropical fever—running hot one second but chilled to the bone next. And now the world pitched beneath her feet. She reached out for something to balance. The worst sea swells were nothing on this sudden rockiness.

'Maia?' he snapped.

His arms were around her again and it was such a relief that she collapsed, leaning in and letting him take her weight.

'Maia?' A gentler question this time. More like the promise he'd made to her early this morning when she'd not known who he was.

She'd missed this feeling of being safe in his embrace. As if she'd found safe harbour. Yet it was madness because she knew it was a lie. The last thing she was here was *safe*. Anger surged—raw and unstoppable—and the words spilled before she could think to stop them.

'This child is *mine*. I am its mother and I will be raising it.'

Her mother had left her and she would never, ever do that to her own child. So she lifted her head and furiously flung her position in his face. 'You want this child, you get me too.'

'Fine,' he snapped right back at her. 'But if this child is mine then you get *me* too.'

He glared right into her eyes. Only inches apart that faint scent of the sea and that disturbingly good spice seduced her. She felt his biceps flex and the awful thing was that with his body pressed against hers she felt even more faint. All she wanted was to stay leaning against him. Heat surged, chasing off the chill that had weakened her only moments before. Everything slowed—her pulse, her breath, time itself. For a long, long moment she gazed back into those beautiful brown eyes, watching as his long lashes half lowered as his focus fell to her mouth. She felt the attention like it were touch. He was closer. Her lips tingled, parted. Deep in her belly she felt the drive to press her hips against his. Her nipples tightened and as she breathed she felt them rub oh so slightly against his hard chest. Desire ignited.

Kiss me.

She gasped, suddenly mortified that she might've muttered the shockingly inappropriate wish aloud.

He blinked, his expression shuttering. 'Are you okay now?'

'Yes,' she mumbled, desperately pushing herself away from him. 'I guess I don't have my land legs yet.'

Anything to excuse that mortifying moment of weakness. Anything to get away from him and be eternally grateful that she'd only said that in her head.

But he made sure she was entirely steady before releasing her.

As he walked to stare out the window, Maia gave herself a mental slap—*pull it together*.

Niko hadn't thought anything fanciful in that moment—he just hadn't wanted her to faint. His concern was wholly on her health and she was making a colossal fool of herself thinking she'd seen otherwise. But the tightness of his hold and the intensity of his gaze upon her had made her senses reel and there *had* been a moment in which he'd leaned closer, breaching polite distance into intimacy. She *hadn't* imagined it. But perhaps it was simply so normal for him he couldn't help himself. He was so practiced at seduction it was second nature and he didn't even realise he was doing it.

'We're in agreement, then,' he said, finally turning back to face her. 'You will stay here. We're forced together through circumstance.'

She hadn't said she would stay here. He had so much more power than she did and she knew too well what it was like to be at the mercy of someone not just bigger and stronger but with connections and money and all of the control. And they were only *forced* together because he was insisting on it.

'What was with the dawn raid?' she challenged him. 'Why couldn't you just phone ahead and then board like normal?'

'We weren't sure of your knowledge of the situation, plus your vessel has evaded authorities in the past,' he answered. 'We expected the operation to be very quick.'

She was an 'operation'. A problem, not a person. And what did he mean by her 'knowledge' of the situation? Had he thought she might be complicit in this catastrophe in some way? How could she have been?

'Obviously now things will change,' he added grimly. 'Your father will be informed of your whereabouts.'

'Don't tell him about the baby.' Agitated by the thought she stepped towards him. 'I don't want you to tell him.'

Her father would not be an ally. He would want to take what *he* could get from this. He wouldn't get it— but the shame of it would be too awful. She had to handle King Niko herself.

'Of course I won't if you don't wish me to,' Niko assured her calmly. 'Frankly I'd prefer that we keep this quiet while we ascertain paternity and then make the necessary arrangements.'

And just what were those necessary arrangements to be?

He watched her keenly. 'If the child is mine, then I am sure we can come to an agreement where you'll be better off than you have been until now.'

That soft, patronising assumption angered her. It wouldn't be an 'agreement' but an order. How could her life be better when she still had little choice in what she did? Now she had less chance of getting her freedom. And as for her poor child?

Bitterness flooded her, forcing a sarcastic snap. 'Wow, you make it sound as if I've won a lottery of some kind and I should be all "hashtag, grateful"!'

CHAPTER THREE

NIKO RUBBED HIS temple and tried to remind himself that the woman before him was still in a state of shock and he needed to be patient. But it was an unusually difficult task. Nobody, but nobody, spoke to him the way she had—repeatedly—in the five minutes since he'd walked into the room. That she'd challenged him about his sex life, her voice vibrating with judgement, had been enough to irritate him, but for her to be so clearly appalled by the generous assurance he was now trying to offer? It was unreasonable. This situation was bad enough without her creating unnecessary drama. It wasn't as if he were thrilled either. Despite being almost thirty he'd had zero intention of marrying any woman anytime soon. He'd have to eventually, but he'd not planned to for a decade more at least. Children would have been minimal. An heir and a spare at most. Having seen his parents' struggles a love match was utterly out of the question and so, as distasteful to him as it was, he'd been preparing for the lesser of two horrors—a passionless arrangement similar to that of his grandparents.

He'd intended to select someone able to handle the challenges of public life, someone who had the upbringing, education and experience to perform the job. Someone from a nearby nation perhaps, but one definitely from a similar level in society as him. That certainly wasn't some young Cinderella who'd spent almost all of her twenty-three years below deck on her father's grimy illegal gambling boat. She was the worst possible option.

So yeah, he wanted to snap back at her and he swerved close to it. But he took a breath and saw how sallow and tired she looked. Like any cornered creature she was lashing out to defend herself. He'd seen Pax's bare bones report—she was virtually a slave for her own father, so he understood why she'd be prickly. He would rise above her aggravation. If he was the father of her baby, he would execute an understanding tolerable to them both. They wouldn't actually have to have much to do with each *other* at all in this.

A muscle in his eyelid twitched and he struggled to stand still. The urge to step forward and fold her into his arms again almost overpowered him. It was flat-out crazy. But she wasn't anything like he'd expected. He'd locked eyes on her just before dawn this morning and seen everything that *hadn't* been visible in the long-range-lens photo in Pax's file. She had midnight eyes, big beautiful orbs that were unfathomably deep and mysterious—the sort a man could lose himself in for aeons and honestly, he had. He'd lost sense of everything for a moment, his purpose—hell, his own name. He'd gazed endlessly, absorbing the height of her, the narrowness of her shoulders, the length of her neck, the fullness of her lips. All her features added up to a beauty that had shaken him. And those hypnotic eyes had simply tempted him.

Now he tried to suppress the empty ache but the contentment he'd felt while holding her for the duration of that journey had been *weird* and worse, he missed it. He'd refused to relinquish her, ignoring the querying looks from Pax. But she was his responsibility and he'd *felt* her fear. It had been imperative that he try to reassure her somehow, even slightly. He had the desire to do that again now. Problem was that desire was being diluted by another even stronger one.

No. It was probably just the uncertainty of the situation pushing him to literally take charge of her. Basic instincts often generated physical actions, right? Like lust. He would ignore it. She needed reassurance only, not unbridled seduction.

'Perhaps you should be grateful,' he said quietly. 'After all, you might not have known the truth of your condition for some time and that could've brought complications for you. At the very least you'll now get the medical attention you need.'

It's your job to look after her. His father's words echoed in his mind and he tensed. He would not fail this time.

'And whether the child you carry is mine or not, I promise you'll continue to receive the care you need throughout this pregnancy and beyond.' He stepped closer, unable to resist that urge to be nearer, needing to impress upon her his uncompromising position. 'But let me also promise that *my* firstborn will be the heir to my throne, regardless of their gender. My firstborn will have everything that is rightfully theirs. *Everything*. Honour. Riches. Protection. And my name.'

Despite his distaste for marriage he would ensure the legitimacy of this child. Secrets and shame had destroyed too much of his family already. It was never happening again.

She swallowed. 'Your name?'

'We'll marry as soon as the paternity is confirmed.' He saw panic swoop into her eyes. 'In name only,' he added swiftly. 'While you're pregnant.'

'But then?' She stared at him in consternation. 'No king of Piri-nu has ever divorced.'

He hesitated. It was bitterly unfortunate and of course he dreaded condemning someone to palace life for good but he had no choice.

His aunt Lani had been illegitimate—the firstborn offspring of his philandering grandfather. She'd been reared within the palace walls but her lineage not just unacknowledged, but hidden. She'd worked as a maid and had unknowingly served her own blood relatives. The devastation that had ensued when the truth came out was something Niko had never forgiven himself for. And he would never allow anything like it to happen again.

He would do better for this child. Maybe he would even allow them to make their own decision regarding claiming the crown eventually. Maia could have choices too. Initially they would be limited but beyond the birth, he would assist her however he could.

'There will be support and more freedom than you think,' he said.

She was pretty and with new clothes she might be

stunning. And while she had zero society training, that could be provided. Except even with all that, Niko knew how hard someone could find palace life. Somehow he had to come up with something satisfactory. He just didn't know what it was yet.

Divorce would only be a last resort.

'Are you saying I have to marry you and finish growing your baby but then I'll be free to live my life however I please?' she pushed him.

'There will be certain limitations.'

'Such as?'

The defiance in her eyes set his teeth on edge. 'We're getting ahead of ourselves,' he gritted out, barely reining in his temper. 'Perhaps we need to wait for the paternity results before finalising our marriage details.'

She stared at him in horror all over again. 'How long will it take to get those?'

'I'll get the doctor. I believe he brought the necessary equipment.' He saw her flinch and felt a flash of compunction. 'You'll be okay, Maia. I promise you he is our best.'

He didn't return to the room with the doctor. Maia needed privacy and he needed time to think. But he paced right outside, oddly anxious as he waited for the examination to be completed. He needed to know she was well enough to withstand this pregnancy. He'd asked the doctor to make very sure of that. Because right now she didn't *look* it and she'd had that near fainting spell. But then he remembered the fight in her body when he'd grabbed her this morning—her lithe agility and defiance. She had spirit and strength when she needed it. And if she had proper support then they might get through this.

He whirled when the door opened. 'Everything okay?'

'I'm going to do an ultrasound scan to check the foetus,' the doctor said. 'I wondered if you would like to observe.'

Niko hesitated. When Pax had first come to him with concern in his face and told him about a possible mix-up at the medical centre, Niko had thought he was pranking him. It was the most preposterous thing he'd ever heard. He, like Maia, had laughed. It was a catalogue of coincidences impossible to believe.

Pax was tracking down information about who'd been scheduled for the insemination and how it was that his sample had been used. He didn't yet know if there were sinister implications but in all this he'd never believed that such a random procedure would have been successful. The doctor had added false reassurance too. After all, it would have had to have been the right time for Maia. Apparently it had been and he might just have to step up and become a father. The one thing he'd never wanted to do, alongside a woman he didn't know at all and who wasn't the right kind of woman destined to be his bride.

Unless, of course, she was already pregnant by another man and this baby wasn't *his* at all. Yet oddly, that prospect made him unaccountably angrier and yes, he realised he would like to observe the scan. He wanted to see Maia's face.

'Thank you.' He nodded.

Back in the lounge Maia was reclined on the sofa.

Her trousers were loosened and tugged down only enough to reveal her belly. He averted his gaze from the paler skin and gentle curve. She'd turned her face away and didn't acknowledge his arrival. He suppressed the sudden urge to cup her cheek and gently turn her back to him. Her avoidance bothered him not because it was a blatant disregard of protocol, but because it felt more personal. He felt she disliked him. Oddly— because it really shouldn't matter—he disliked *that* realisation intensely.

He glanced down and saw she'd balled her hand into a fist. He saw the purpling patch on her wrist from when she'd hit it as she'd almost slipped in trying to get away from him. Shame licked his insides. Plus her lips were puffier and redder because of the tape they'd sealed across her mouth. He'd noticed it when she'd had that dizzy spell just before—that pout had been appallingly tempting. Regret filled him. Whether this was his baby or not, this woman needed better care.

He focused on the portable monitor as the doctor slid a wand over Maia's stomach. For a moment it was all grey swirls. Then it was there. A blob. Then identifiable parts—head, limbs, *life*. The heartbeat sounded like galloping ponies.

'That's fast.' He glanced at the doctor in concern. 'Is that—'

'Perfectly normal, Your Highness,' the doctor calmly replied without taking his assessing gaze from the screen. 'Everything is looking very well. The measurements look appropriate for the time of the original appointment and the foetus is developing well.'

So it was the right size, right stage of development

to be *his*. He glanced back at Maia's face. She'd been looking at the screen as well and now she looked at him and he saw the truth in her eyes. This was *his* child. Even as she lifted her chin in slight defiance. He was suddenly certain there was no boyfriend. His possible bride was not promiscuous. Her disapproval of his sexual mores echoed in his ears. Yet he'd also seen the flare in her eyes when he'd held her close through that dizziness. And he'd felt her response. It hadn't been fear. It hadn't been distaste. It had been heat. Temptation curled. Niko Ture was used to being well regarded and if he had to win over his reluctant bride he knew one way to do it.

No. This wasn't about proving a point or about personal *pleasure*. No doubt that was what she expected of him and he was filled with the desire to behave contrary to her disapproving expectations. They were going to have to get along for a lifetime which meant instead of seducing her, he might have to make her his friend. But Niko had few true friends. He didn't trust many people and the likelihood of him trusting her?

He sighed. She would be a business partner at best. Ideally a distant acquaintance. The palace was large enough for them to reside in effectively separate households. But that didn't get around the fact that his people were going to demand much that she didn't yet understand.

What had happened at that clinic was a mistake, maybe. A miracle, definitely. It was the most appalling complication of his adult life.

He ushered the doctor out, speaking with him briefly in the corridor to arrange a full debrief later. And to get something he needed now. When he returned she'd tidied her clothing and was awkwardly perched on the edge of the sofa. He drew up a small footstool and sat before her, smiling to himself when her eyes widened.

He squeezed ointment from the tube he'd gotten from the doctor.

'What are you doing?' she asked.

He held his hand out for her to put hers in. 'May I?'

Maia stared, confused by his gesture and intention and that soft smile. Confused because she'd just seen proof of a tiny life growing within her on that screen. Confused because she had no idea what she should do next. There was too much to process—that she was pregnant was truly a miracle she couldn't yet believe. For so long she'd secretly feared that would be impossible—not just because she'd thought she might never have her freedom to find a partner but that she might not have the physical capacity for pregnancy even if she did. But now there was absolute contrariness—amazement and incredulity and *wonder*...

All her weak body wanted was to tip back into this *stranger's* arms and cry—both scared tears and happy tears. But Maia never cried and she wasn't about to start now.

'Your wrist.' He nodded simply. 'It's bruised.'

'But you don't need to—'

'Please. It's herbal, it won't harm the baby.'

She was stunned he was thinking of the child's well-being so efficiently already. But as she stared, she absorbed his calmness and slowly that half smile compelled her. Suppressing her embarrassment she put her hand in his. She knew to him it meant nothing. He was used to touch. But *she* wasn't and it took everything in her not to shiver when he carefully clasped her hand.

He rubbed the ointment onto her wrist with soft strokes. Maia stared at his long fingers as he rhythmically soothed the grazed skin and she tensed, desperate not to tremble in response. He was more gentle than she'd ever have expected and the sensations stirring within her were too intimate.

'I'm sorry you were hurt,' he said huskily after a few moments. 'It was the last thing I wanted to happen.'

'That was my best knife,' she muttered awkwardly. 'But I can get it when I go back.'

He glanced up briefly before focusing on her wrist again. The starkness of this situation became clear.

Was she *ever* going to go back? Her lungs tightened. No more staying below deck on her feet for hours, making snacks for gambling guests. But she would be stuck *here* instead. With this man. As his bride.

His touch suddenly sizzled and she swiftly pulled her hand free.

He sat still, silent, apparently all understanding and patience.

She had to do better. Thinking quickly, she quelled the tremble in her hands enough to lift the uncapped tube he'd placed beside her on the sofa and took a dab of ointment. Then she held her hand out for his.

She heard him catch his breath but she didn't lift her gaze to meet his eyes. She had no hope of compelling him with a look the way he had her. If she looked at him she would lose courage and she needed to show her equality to him in this. Here and now at least.

His hesitation was momentary before he put his hand

in hers. It was so much bigger and she rested it in her lap. She lightly stroked the fleshy base of his thumb, smearing the fresh-smelling ointment over the part where her teeth had left a faint mark.

'I meant to hurt you,' she admitted softly.

'I know,' he said. 'I don't blame you. I would have done the same.'

She stared at the strong hand that dwarfed both of hers, seeing the smooth copper tone of his skin, the neatly trimmed nails. It was beautiful hand—like the rest of him. And it was heavy. It held such power.

'I understand why you did what you did.' She finally glanced up and braved those brown eyes that saw so much. 'Still think you could have just called ahead.'

'Would that really have been wise?'

She couldn't stand the hint of sympathy in his expression. He thought he knew things about her. But he knew nothing.

His hand was warm on her lap. But this tenderness wasn't real and the instinct to reject its blossoming facade burned. But before she could say anything more he lifted his fingers and touched her lower lip ever so gently, tripling the sense of intimacy.

'I'm sorry about this too,' he muttered.

Her lips throbbed at his touch and sent a searing shot of desire all the way to her belly. But she kept looking into his eyes. 'You silenced me.'

'Yes.' His hand dropped. 'I had no choice.'

No choice but to take away *her* choices. And he was going to do it again, wasn't he? Sorry or not, he was still going to do it.

'There are always choices,' she argued. 'Can't you

just make a proclamation of some kind? To make the baby your heir without us having to… You're the *king*.'

Didn't he have all the power?

'And not even a king can change some things,' he said. 'There can be no question of my child's validity. Their rights. What's happened is not this baby's fault and they'll not suffer anything adverse because of it. I'll do whatever it takes to protect them from any possible harm.'

Would he protect them even from their own mother if he considered her to be a threat? Maia felt his conviction and understood. She could be within his circle. Or she could be on the outside. That was the only 'choice' that was hers. He held all the cards. The child would be born here and be the new heir to Piri-nu.

But Maia had protective instincts of her own. This was a child she'd not been sure she'd ever be able to have. So she too would do whatever was required to protect her or him from any possible harm.

Being separated from a mother caused harm.

Having one's life completely controlled caused harm.

So she needed to buy time to think everything through. To make her own plans.

'Well.' She attempted a small, pacifying smile. 'I suppose we need to wait for the results of the paternity test before making all the decisions anyway.'

He blinked.

'I'd like to rest now,' she added. 'I'm very tired.'

'Of course.' But he looked at her searchingly for a moment. 'Would you like a tray sent up? Some pineapple juice perhaps?'

She'd spilled her juice when he'd appeared. He'd remembered the sort. Which meant he noticed things. Small things. Maybe *all* things. Which made her even more wary. If she'd thought it impossible to escape her father, Niko would be even harder.

'No, thank you,' she muttered.

'Well, if you think of anything all you have to do is push this button and someone will come to attend to you.' He pointed out the small call button.

'It's like a five-star hotel,' she joked wanly. 'I can order room service.'

'You can order anything you want.'

Anything. She heard a hint of huskiness and something rippled deep inside. But she refused to let her mind wander into that dangerous territory and reminded herself that she was the one usually answering such summonses—waking up to make fresh brioche for roaringly drunk, starving guests at two in the morning. Now she could make someone else do that for her if she wished. It was the last thing she'd do.

'Anything except my freedom,' she said softly.

'Yes.' He nodded. 'Except that.'

She regarded him sombrely. 'Thank you for your generosity.'

She meant it. But her freedom—and that of her baby—was the one thing she was going to fight for.

CHAPTER FOUR

IT WAS A relief when he left. Her brain—annoyingly sluggish in his presence—came back online. She didn't have time to indulge in self-pity—she had her escape to plan. She needed every ounce of energy to *think*. Because no way was she marrying that man. Not *any* man. Well, not for the next five years at least. She'd dreamed of her freedom for too long. She wanted to explore, to study, to carve out a career that she chose for *herself*.

She wasn't being tied to a future held within someone else's control. And a king was used to being in complete control of his whole world. He said he wanted her to have choices but that was a polite platitude. She knew exactly what it was like to live with a dictator and she wasn't about to swap one for another.

But she was pregnant. She'd just *seen* that baby in black and white on the screen. It was impossible to believe. But it was also *amazing*.

And of course the child should know its world, its heritage, its father. But Maia didn't need to *marry* him in order for that to happen. Niko's view was insanely old-fashioned and of course understandable because he was king. But he needed to learn he couldn't control her.

She wasn't going to agree to everything he decreed the second he spoke. And he expected that.

If she didn't stand up to him, if she didn't get some strength here, she would be in a worse position than ever before. So she needed to make her stand now. She needed to get space and time so he understood that she too would have some power in her position.

Then there was the mortifying fact she was sexually attracted to him. Had discovering she was carrying his baby heightened her awareness of his sensuality? Was it some basic instinct to want him—some gut drive to protect the unexpected child within her?

Except it had happened in that first moment when she'd turned and seen him standing there. He'd been completely unrecognisable yet she'd felt an instant passion tug within—

Surely it wasn't that. Surely she was mistaking the adrenalin surge of fear for attraction. She was confused, that was all.

But there'd been so many moments since then. Every time he got within two feet of her she felt her arousal rising. It was awful and she needed to get a grip.

She moved. One door led to the bathroom, one to the corridor, but she'd yet to investigate that third. She opened it and glanced in. The bed was the first thing she saw. Clad in luxuriously soft-looking white linen, it was huge. She quickly shut the door again, her heart thumping. She'd never slept on a bed like that. She'd never *seen* a bed like that. And it was most definitely big enough for two. Hell, for three or four or more…was that what he was used to? Heat washed over her face.

She scurried back to the sofa and curled up on it,

trying to figure out what she could do. Trying to figure out how on earth any of this could have happened. Had someone planned to impregnate themselves with him as the father? The ramifications were appalling—that someone might want to use that against him was frightening because he was a powerful man. It didn't seem likely anyone would be so bold. But he was right, that part wasn't her problem. It was his. She had enough to deal with. The air was still scented with that herbal ointment and it was surprisingly soothing. As she sat—failing to formulate any kind of plan at all—the last of that adrenalin drained out and the fatigue that had plagued her these last few weeks hit again. At least now she knew the reason for it. Her eyelids felt heavy. She closed them. She was not going to cry. Not ever.

She had no idea what time it was when she woke. Truthfully she could sleep hours longer but that wasn't an option. She had work to do. She needed to go on a reconnaissance mission and figure out whether any escape was even remotely possible. But she had some hope because Piri-nu was prosperous and its population was content and proud of its king. She'd never known of any civil unrest here, so fingers crossed palace security wasn't as tight as it might be in other places. Maybe those guards might be a little complacent. Only then she remembered the efficiency with which they'd extracted her from her father's boat. Still, she had to try. She opened the door that Niko had used. She quickly walked the length of the wide corridor but when she turned the corner she encountered a severe-looking guard coming her way. She froze. He was beef-cake muscles enormous and scary and the aviator sunglasses didn't hide the fact he was glaring at her and could probably see straight through to all her guilty plans.

'Is there something you need, ma'am?' he asked.

She hesitated, thrown by being called ma'am. 'Is it okay if I go for a short walk in the gardens?'

He paused for a second as if waiting on someone else's response. 'Would you like me to escort you?'

She shook her head. 'No, thank you, they're just down those stairs?'

He inclined his head and she walked past, faking confidence. He hadn't actually refused her.

At the bottom of the stairs she passed another soldier who didn't so much as blink as she walked past. But she saw the earpiece he wore. So perhaps that first guy had radioed him to let him know it was okay.

Outside she realised it was later in the day than she'd thought. The gardens were lush but the air was heavy and hot.

'You have your land legs back now?' a sardonic query came from behind her.

Her pulse picked up. So he'd been summoned. Was it the guard in the corridor or were there cameras that were too well hidden for her to have spotted? It had to be the guard. The king had better things to do than watch a security feed all day.

'Apparently so,' she mumbled, turning to him. 'I seem to have slept almost all day, I needed to stretch out a little and test them.'

They weren't the only things she was testing. She'd glanced at the high fences and the ornately carved gates at the nearest part of the palace perimeter and seen that the carvings would make good footholds. Maia was good at scrambling up and down narrow ladders and spaces. Now she just had to keep her brain on track while in Niko's presence.

'What about food—have you had anything to eat since you woke?' Niko paused and cocked his head. 'Will you dine with me tonight?'

There was a commanding thread that undermined the 'optional' element of his invitation. Maia braced. 'If you don't mind, I'd like to retire to my room and have a small tray there. I've got a lot to process.'

Niko stared, then slowly nodded. 'Of course, I understand. Another time.'

'Thank you.' She swallowed.

She'd thought he wouldn't be used to anyone turning him down about anything and his almost immediate acceptance seemed a little off. But then it dawned on her—he probably didn't desire to dine with her at all. He'd been making an effort that he was happy to be saved from. After all they had *nothing* in common and their paths never would have crossed if it weren't for this crazy mix-up.

Heat flushed through her all over again and she was glad of the darkening sky.

'But please allow me to accompany you around the garden before you go in,' he said.

She was still wary of his too agreeable, too innocent tone. But it would be too rude to refuse him something that ought to be innocuous. She could still scope out all she needed to under the guise of awed enthusiasm. 'Of course.'

'The gates were hand-carved more than a century

ago.' He glanced at her as she startled. 'You seemed interested in them.'

'The whole palace is very beautiful,' she hurriedly gushed. 'The whole island.'

'Indeed. All of them. The whole country in fact,' he replied mockingly.

She gritted her teeth.

In this season dusk barely lasted before full darkness fell and it was often heralded by brief intense storms that blew through, cleansing the stifling humidity with a downpour of rain. But today's storm hadn't yet happened and the heaviness in the air pressed upon her skin. Tension built both inside and out of her—making it impossible to breathe or to think properly. The heat was too much.

He suddenly led her diagonally across the springy lawn and stopped by a small side door that she'd not noticed. 'If you go through here and up those stairs it will take you straight to your corridor. It's faster and you'll avoid the weather that's about to hit.'

She stared at the door. It was small and unobtrusive and perfect and she couldn't believe he'd shown her exactly what she needed. 'Thank you.'

But Niko didn't step aside to let her pass, instead he looked down at her. She was at a disadvantage, not only in stature and strength, power and money, but now in illumination. Because while the interior lights shone through onto her face, he had his back to them and thus remained in shadow. So his expression was impossible to read in the sinking darkness while her face was visible. She felt that heat inside wanting to burst. She stared at him almost fixedly, determined to mask her inner turmoil. She would not fall beneath his sensual spell again.

'Good night, Maia. Please eat and then sleep well. I have the feeling we're going to have lots to settle tomorrow. But I hope we'll be able to agree on the things that matter most.'

Her throat clogged unexpectedly. Perhaps he was trying to do the right thing, but it wasn't enough for her. She made herself nod, unable to answer verbally. Because tomorrow she wasn't going to be here.

Twenty minutes later Niko stood beside Pax and studied the screen. 'What did she order to eat?'

'Salad. Fish.'

Niko smiled at Pax's sparse reply and watched her sitting on that sofa again. He regretted the fear he'd made her feel first thing this morning but there'd been no other way given the secrecy this situation required. *Delicate* wasn't the only word. There was *danger* here too. If people had planned to take advantage of the sample that had been stored at that clinic, then they must be aware of her existence now. That meant she might be at risk. The child might be at risk. He didn't want to scare her any more than she had been but she was *safest* here at the palace. With him.

He'd spoken with the doctor at length and now he shifted, needing to pace, as angry energy rippled. What the man had told him added layers of complication to the mess they already faced. And made his care of her all the more crucial.

But *she* wasn't pacing, wasn't crying. She'd done neither of those things all day. She was still, deep in contemplation. Not taking advantage of any of the entertainments available in the room—neither the books nor the screens with several streaming services. Not the offer of a massage or any kind of relaxation treatments. She just sat.

Pax glanced at another of the security feeds. 'She slept for eleven hours solid.'

'Yeah.' More anger rippled through Niko. She'd curled up on the sofa, too exhausted to bother making it to the bedroom. She'd been so still it had been unnerving. He'd found himself checking on her, here in Pax's office, far too many times through the day. Just to make sure she was actually still breathing. To make sure she was still there. There weren't cameras in the bathroom or bedroom of course. There was no need given there was no way to escape from either of those rooms without coming through the small lounge where she now sat. When she'd finally woken she'd disappeared into the bathroom for a while, returning having clearly showered. He'd felt a ridiculous speck of disappointment that he'd still been unable to see her hair. While the fabric covering had gone, she'd swept her still-wet hair back into a bun at the nape of her neck so it was still impossible to determine anything much about it, including length and colour. She was still in those black trousers and that worn shirt. He should have arranged a wardrobe for her but he'd been so preoccupied processing the consequences of her pregnancy he'd not thought of it until late this afternoon. An assistant was on the job now. Tomorrow he would start over with her. Or so he'd intended—until he'd seen her just before.

'She's not going to stay,' Niko muttered grimly. 'She's going to run.'

'You're sure?' Pax asked. 'She said something?'

Niko shook his head with a jerky movement, unable to explain how he knew, just that he did. His sixth sense screamed certainty. When they were outside Maia Flynn had stared him down. There'd been no coy look, no flirtation, not even a demure lowering of her lashes. No subservient mark of respect for her king. That wasn't how she saw him at all. But it was as if he'd momentarily seen into her mind. He just *knew* she was going to attempt an escape. So he'd given her information that would help. Just to see.

For once Pax removed his sunglasses and bent nearer to glare at the screen. 'I'll go—'

'No.' Niko felt that primitive rush of responsibility. She was *his* problem. 'I'll follow her if she leaves the palace. I want to see how she plays this. Don't let anyone interfere with her progress.' He watched her gaze flicker to the window. To that view of the water. 'I think she'll go to what she knows,' he mused quietly. 'She'll go to the dock. She'll try to get on a boat. She'll go before dawn. Allow it.'

Pax nodded slowly. 'I'll ensure we have people there. We'll make sure she's okay. We won't lose her.'

'I know we won't,' Niko said grimly. There would be no repetition of history here. No emotional, desperate journeys. Accidents happened when emotions were heightened—it was what had happened to his aunt after all. And his mother.

But he needed to know how far Maia would go. It piqued him, that she would lie and plot. That she was so appalled at the prospect of staying here with him that she would put herself at risk made his hackles rise. What did she expect? That he would allow a possible heir to the throne to just leave? *He* was trying his best in what was an appalling situation for them both. That she'd consider running away was unacceptable. But, a little voice whispered within, wasn't it *understandable*?

No. There was too much at risk. Too much that was important.

He would give her a little rope and if she ran, then he'd tie her all the more tightly. That was in the best interests of all of them. He could not see another in his family suffer by being outcast from the palace circle.

Yet still he felt for her—she didn't want this life with him and she didn't even have the motivation his mother had had when she'd married his father—and that hadn't worked. Even love was not enough.

'Here's the knife she dropped.' Pax suddenly turned to him and almost smiled. 'I retrieved it while you were in the midst of that scuffle.'

Niko ignored the rare tease from Pax and regarded the small knife thoughtfully. It was smaller than he'd realised, more like a fruit parer. But while the blade was small, it was sharp. And apparently it was her favourite. For what, and why?

'Thank you for that. Good.' He took it and weighed it in his palm.

Pax jerked his chin at the little bruise on Niko's hand. 'Not like you to hesitate and get caught.'

'It's not like me to jump innocent women,' Niko growled back grimly.

But in truth that hesitation had been more than the

distaste of the situation. She'd had her back to him, bending over that knife, but when she'd turned he'd seen the shine in her midnight eyes and there'd been that moment, a jolt of recognition—not of name, or status, but something far more elemental.

The shock of it had rendered him immobile. But in a flash *she'd* been all limbs, all fury as she tried to get away. As she'd slipped. He *still* couldn't forget the sensation of holding her in his arms as he'd stopped her fall. Of locking her between his legs, feeling her lithe lusciousness. Of knowing her in a way he'd never expected to. He should not have felt aroused in any way given how inappropriate and extreme those measures had been. Yet he had been. When he'd then held her close on the journey it wasn't for control, but for her comfort. For his own comfort too. He'd wanted her to understand that she was safe. When he'd finally felt her body relax into his it had brought him a satisfaction unlike any other.

He pocketed the knife and turned back to the screen as thunder hit. She didn't so much as flinch. She was too focused on whatever it was she was thinking. Niko also ignored the rain drumming noisily on the roof. He was going to find out what she had planned, no matter what.

Exhilaration rose at the prospect of duelling with her again. Because she *was* going to challenge him and he was so ready for it.

CHAPTER FIVE

THE DOCK WAS eerily quiet—not even the song and swoop of birdlife disturbed it. It was as if the birds too were holding their breath in solidarity with Maia. She walked quickly, used to being unobtrusive and unnoticed. She'd covered her hair and kept her head down. Given that her freedom depended on this, her adrenalin was stratospheric for the second time in twenty-four hours. She had to succeed because it wasn't only her life on the line. It was her child's as well. Nothing mattered more than ensuring her baby's liberty.

Escaping the palace had been surprisingly easy. There'd been no guard on her door and none on that side door through which she'd gotten into the garden. The carved wooden gate was small and, again, both unlocked and unguarded—or at least able to be opened from the inside. It had taken less than two minutes in that time just before dawn—when the sky was lightening but the world still—to get onto the street and disappear around the corner. It had to be because no one would dream of hurting the king, right? The man was too popular and the city too safe for them to need round-the-clock guards with guns.

She felt a flicker of guilt at abusing the trust he'd bestowed upon her by not having literally locked her away. She believed him when he said he didn't mean to harm her and that he wanted to do what was best. But he also thought *he* knew best and that she would simply agree to everything *he* wanted. But Maia could never sign her life over to him. Her mother had gone from one controlling man to another and she wasn't making the same mistake. In order for things to move forward she needed to reclaim something to negotiate with and honestly the only power she could think of was that of her own placement—literally *where* she was. If she was out of reach, then she had some chance.

The walk to the dock took forever but the sky was barely lightening by the time she got there. The exhilaration from her palace escape faded as the most challenging bit lay ahead. A number of fishermen were preparing their boats to depart for the daily catch. She only needed one to say yes. Her heart thudded.

Take it easy, act like this is normal.

Because it was. It was how most islanders moved around islands outside of ferry hours.

'Any chance of a lift to the next island?' she asked the older man at the first boat.

'Not stopping there, sorry.' He glanced at her for a moment. 'Try Tai further on the dock. White stripe. He's heading to Mica first.'

'Thanks.'

Mica was only two islands up the Piri-nu archipelago but it was a start. She took a steadying breath feeling more vulnerable than she'd ever felt in her life but she straightened her shoulders. No one knew her—or the secret she carried. She was still dressed like a worker. Which was exactly what she was.

'Tai?' She addressed the man with his back to her.

He turned and she blinked. He was younger than she'd expected. But she saw the glint of a wedding band and the distinct—usual—lack of interest in his gaze. 'Any chance I can get a lift to your first stop?'

If she could get to one island, she could then get another boat and could hop her way through. The sooner she got to the first, the better chance she had. No one knew she was missing yet and she was sure King Niko wouldn't want a scandal given he'd gone to such lengths to ensure her arrival at the palace was unknown.

'It's a ninety-minute run,' Tai said bluntly. 'Do you get seasick?'

She stiffened. 'Not usually.'

'Can you help with the ropes at the stern?'

'Of course.'

'Then step on board.'

She studied the boat as she did. It was old but well maintained. Safe enough in this weather. She headed to the front of the boat, eager to help them get moving before her disappearance was discovered. Hopefully she had a couple hours yet before one of those maids appeared with a dining tray.

The boat rocked as she moved forward but she felt the ripple of freedom. She released the line then coiled the rope neatly. The boat manoeuvred away from the dock. It seemed the young fisherman was keen to get underway too. She remained at the stern, looking towards the sea as the engine chugged, getting them out of the inner harbour and hoping the next phase would go as smoothly. She was finally enacting the desperate escape scenario she'd imagined from her father's boat for years but never had the courage to attempt before now. Ultimately she would aim for somewhere as far as New Zealand or Australia. Once she was there she'd try to get a job in a cafe. If she could find someone to give her a chance she was sure she could prove herself. It wouldn't be for that long of course. She had no intention of hiding from Niko forever. She just needed time and space to figure out how to manage *him*.

'Where is it we're going, Maia?'

She closed her eyes, rooted to the spot.

Of course it was too good to be true. Of course it had been too easy.

She heard a splash and reluctantly turned, opening her eyes in time to see Tai—if that was even his name— swimming to shore. Leaving her alone with her captor king looking at her with condemnation in his deep brown eyes.

Well, she wasn't going to cower before him and apologise. It was his own fault for assuming so much yesterday. As if she *ever* wanted to be his queen? As if she ever could do as she was ordered for the rest of her life? As if she could let her child *see* her do that?

'How did you know which boat I was going to choose?' she asked.

'I didn't. I had a man on all of them.'

Her stomach knotted. 'You followed me from the palace.'

'You even used the door I showed you.'

So he'd predicted her every move, and the barely leashed fury in his eyes revealed the temper that could explode at any moment. And wasn't he justified in that? Could she really blame him?

She'd thought she'd been so brilliant but all she'd done was poke the bear and now things would only be worse. 'Are we not turning round immediately?'

'We are not,' he said. 'You've just proven that I cannot trust you, Maia. So now we change the plan.'

She chilled. 'You've sent the fisherman away.'

'The *soldier* away, yes. But you can trust me. I can steer this boat.'

'So can I.' She suddenly lifted her chin in brave— possibly foolish—defiance. 'So if you happened to go overboard in the middle of the ocean I could journey on and find my freedom forever.'

'Are you threatening the king?' He laughed briefly— bitterly—before stepping close. 'Would you want such an accident to befall the father of your child?'

She stared back up at him, provoked into pushing him back however she could. 'What makes you certain you're the father all of a sudden? I thought you weren't getting the test results—'

'I know you're a virgin, Maia.'

The statement stunned her. She stared up at him awash with shock, then anger, then such overwhelming embarrassment that she couldn't speak.

His expression changed. 'The doctor examined you yesterday, remember?' he asked—his voice slightly more gentle, slightly husky.

'But that was for—' The horror of her total humiliation hit. She hadn't realised that the doctor would have been able to tell or that he would have even considered to look for such a thing. She'd thought that physical exam had been to assess the pregnancy, not her personal *status*...

It was such a horrible violation of her privacy. And she was so stupidly naive and clueless on all these things. She burned, blinking rapidly even though her eyes were dry. Her mother flashed into her mind and Maia's fury bloomed brighter still. She wasn't only hurt that her mother had abandoned her but angry because Maia had been left so ignorant as a result. And for that doctor to have told the king something that was so personal, so private, so awkward—

'You've really been enjoying yourself at my expense, haven't you?' She gasped.

'Not at all,' Niko answered directly, his unapologetic gaze fixed upon her. 'It was a tangential discovery, Maia. He wasn't deliberately investigating that aspect of your...life.' For a moment he actually looked awkward. 'Given that discovery though, he opted not to perform the DNA test. Especially because he said you'd suffered abnormal pain for a long time. He said that was why you sought treatment that day.' He paused. 'But you'd not tried to get help for it earlier.'

He paused again but Maia simply couldn't speak. It hadn't been easy when she lived on the boat so much. That appointment had been a cancellation. She'd thought she'd been *lucky*.

'While the DNA test will still be done at some point, we both already know the result. He and I agree there is no need to subject you to further testing at this stage.'

Was she supposed to be *grateful* for that? Because she wasn't. She just wanted to curl into a ball and hide.

'The doctor considers it vital that you get rest for this stage of your pregnancy,' he added.

'And the doctor didn't consider telling any of this personal information to me directly?' she asked acidly.

'He would have today if you hadn't run away.'

She gritted her teeth in annoyance. 'But he had no scruples about breaking patient confidentiality and telling *you* already.'

'Because I am the king and these are *exceptional* circumstances. I want only what's best for both you and the baby.' He drew a sharp breath. 'Stress is not what's best.' He looked at her. 'Running away is not what's best.' He turned and went to the wheel.

'And only you know what is best?' She followed him furiously. 'Only you can decide?'

He lifted his chin in a mirror of her defiance. 'Am I such an ogre, Maia?'

She honestly didn't know. But she couldn't cede all power so soon. 'I feel uncomfortable about how much you seem to know about me. I feel like you've had people pry into my personal life.'

'That's not entirely true. My most trusted security man is the only one to have made inquiries. Then it is only the medical centre and the doctor. I am trying to protect your privacy as best I can. That is why I removed you from the boat in the way that I did.'

'It leaves me feeling violated. Nothing is mine.'

'Your thoughts are your own.' His eyes flashed. 'Your body too.'

'Is that so?' She stared at him mutinously. 'You're saying I can go anywhere and do anything?'

His jaw clamped. 'I meant in an intimate capacity.

You don't need to fear anything from me. I know you think I'm some kind of player but—'

'I get it.' Her petulant ego didn't need to hear yet another time about how little he was attracted to her. She was safe from any sexual attention from him. Fine. Great.

'Right, so you seem to think you know a lot about me too, correct?' he said. 'People pry into my personal life all the time. I'm saying I understand the discomfort of that sensation.'

'You're the king, it comes with the job.'

'Yes,' he said soberly. 'It does. This isn't what *either* of us wanted. You need time to process the situation. You need rest. You need to be safe.'

Safe from *what* exactly?

'So now you're taking me where—to some kind of prison?' she asked sarcastically.

His jaw tensed. Why succeeding in angering him gave her small satisfaction she didn't know. She'd never been this shrewish before. But then she'd never been impossibly pregnant and kidnapped by a king before either.

All Niko wanted was to do the right thing but it seemed no matter what he did or how he framed it, she found fault and flared up. And in turn, well, he was rapidly heading towards nuclear. Both the failure to soothe her and his response was unusual. He'd seen Pax's report so he hadn't been going into this situation completely blind and yet he'd still managed to blow it. Since when was he so lacking in charm? He convinced people to do his bidding all the damned time without having to actually order them.

Maia Flynn had lived all her life on a vessel that could sink at any time. Like some low-level casino cruise, they voyaged around the Pacific, taking passengers into international waters for illegal high-stakes gambling. Her father had been investigated several times but never charged. Certainly never convicted. Maia worked in the galley not just full-time, but literally every hour she was awake.

Didn't she realise she never had to work again if she didn't want to? That she would have all the riches of the world—that she could live a refined, relaxed life in the palace? Wasn't that better than what she'd endured all her life so far?

So why had the thought of staying with him been so repellent that she'd felt forced to run away first thing this morning?

He'd never intended to throw the fact of her virginity in her face. He'd not even been going to bring it up. It was too personal. But inexplicably he'd gotten so mad at the mere sight of her, he'd snapped. There was no denying the veracity of the doctor's finding—her immediate expression had confirmed it all. But he wasn't about to tell her the other things the doctor had told him at the time. That he was 'fine to sleep with her'— just to 'be gentle and take it slow.' Niko had furiously changed the topic. He did not need guidance on bedroom performance from a doctor. Besides which it was irrelevant because he was never going to be intimate with Maia Flynn. He would install her on his private holiday island with his most loyal servant in safety and she would want for nothing. Ever. He would make it so damn heavenly she'd never want to leave.

His long-dormant protective instincts had surged. He'd not realised they were so strong. This wasn't only about the baby, this was about her. She had medical issues that hadn't been diagnosed properly, and she'd not had the care she should have had. All that was going to change. Rest. No stress. Nutritious food. These things he could supply. He could make life more than good for her. This wouldn't be anything like what had happened to his aunt. He could do a better job than his grandfather ever had. And he would damn well do a better job of looking after her than he had looked after his mother.

So seducing Maia wasn't on that list. But awareness crackled and a wicked whisper constantly suggested he get closer. She was the one woman he shouldn't touch. But for some unknown reason she was the one he wanted more than his next breath. It was such a cliché to want something simply because it wasn't allowed. That's all this was, right? The temptation of forbidden fruit.

Well, he would resist and dismiss that temptation. He would keep his distance and encourage her to accept what was going to happen. They would have a marriage of convenience, not intimacy, and she could have all the freedom she wanted out here. She would be alone while their names were still joined. But beyond that—

'We need to press on,' he said abruptly. 'We have quite a way to go.'

As he put the boat into full power he saw a sparkle illuminate her midnight eyes. She clearly loved the water despite the lack of freedom on her father's boat. Being out here in the sunlight, chasing the light winds, moving towards his favourite island, he too felt his mood and energy lift. So he stayed silent, unwilling to debate pointlessly with her about a future that was already settled.

As the sun rose higher she moved around the boat, first tidying the ropes into neater coils, then polishing with a soft cloth she'd found somewhere. As if she couldn't rest. As if she didn't know she didn't have to work anymore.

'You work on deck on your father's boat?' he couldn't resist asking.

'Only sometimes, when we don't have guests. I'm not the best but I know the basics.'

'And of course you have your sea-legs.' He gave in to the temptation to tease. Just a little.

It was a mistake. She shot him a look and despite the distance between them on deck the atmosphere thickened and he felt her challenge as if it were an actual arm wrestle. In seconds he was so close to snatching her into his arms again. When she finally turned away he gritted his teeth and summoned every ounce of restraint he could.

Three hours later Maia stood at the stern keenly seeking more glimpses of the large wooden mansion through the lush palm trees. The sand was pale gold and powdery and in the blue depths below them she could see beautiful coral, colourful fish and her favourites, the turtles.

Her heart pounded as she realised a terrifying—tantalising—truth. 'This is your private island.'

It was small and isolated. They would be alone and

there would be no escape from *him*. And already there'd been that moment when he'd simply looked at her and she'd all but combusted on the spot. A wild feeling swept over her. She needed to get away not just from him but the dangerous direction of her own thoughts— the feeling that she would so easily succumb to the attraction that was so stupid. So inevitable.

'Yes,' he said.

She was glad he'd not berated her more and simply pushed on in silence. He'd surprised her with his boating skills. He knew what he was doing, where he was going. But of course this was literally his world. He'd radioed a couple of times and she'd no doubt they were being tracked. She'd grown hotter and hotter not from the sun but the more time she spent in his company.

'I often swim from here,' he added. 'But I'll get the inflatable for—'

'I can swim,' she snapped. 'I'll see you there.'

Before he could answer—or move—she stretched her arms wide and dived straight in. When she surfaced she heard a long string of cursing from the boat behind her but the instant hit of happiness at being in the ocean was too strong to be squished and she simply laughed. The journey had wrought a tension within that she could no longer stand. She adored the water. She was strong in it. And *free*. Now she swam like it was a race for gold—anticipation making adrenalin surge again. She was almost at the shore when she felt a tug on her leg. She recognised the firm grip. She'd been expecting it. Frankly she was pleased it had taken him as long as it had to catch her. She kicked out and put her feet down.

This near to the beach the water was just above waist deep on her but on him—

She stared as he surfaced right beside her. He was bare-chested. He was also furious. But as that wasn't uncommon it was the bare-chested bit that floored her.

'There are rocks you could have hit when you dived in,' he shouted. '*Why* must you always challenge me, Maia?'

She was too busy absorbing the fact that he'd taken the time to strip to his briefs and still caught up to her to answer immediately. Then she was unable to do anything but stare at the swathes of smooth, copper-toned skin and the sharply defined muscles. She gazed at the stunning circular tattoo across his shoulder while another slid down his ribs to the side of his heart.

'I don't know,' she breathed. But she felt more alive than she had in days, months, hell—*years*. Restless energy fired through her so powerfully that she was desperate to release it.

'Don't you?'

The water lapped and the smallest of waves impacted on her like a tsunami. She stumbled and fell against him.

'Then let me show you,' he growled, his hands instantly going to her waist. He lifted her right off her feet. Maia looped her hands over his shoulders and clasped them together at the nape of his neck. For balance, right? But the action allowed her to be pressed more intimately against his bare chest. He was hot and hard and strong as he pressed her closer until they were plastered together from chest through stomach, hips, thighs. And then mouths.

Mouths most of all.

His lips locked on hers. His tongue flickered into her mouth and entwined with hers. He kissed her increasingly intimately, plundering her mouth with luscious thrusts the way he'd fill that other, aching, empty part inside her. The part that had slickened and heated and that she couldn't help rubbing against him. With power and passion and relentless depth he commanded her response and she gave it all. While her innards went weak, her arms remained strong. Energy flowed through her and she clung to him like a limpet. Mind lost, only instinct remained. And the *hunger*. That all-consuming hunger simply grew. She was not releasing him. She was not ever ending this searing kiss. Pleasure shot through her entirety. She arched her feet, half kicking to keep afloat, to keep every inch sealed to him. Her clothes were sopping and as her shirt was already old and thin it now might as well not exist. She could feel more than her own reaction. She could feel *his* ferocity of passion. It made her quake. She heard his low growl and felt the vibration from his chest through hers as his hand swept down her back and pressed, driving her hips harder against his. She shook even more then as his fierce erection jutted against her. She parted her legs to let him fit better, nearer to where she wanted his touch most. His hand tightened on her hip, grinding her on him.

Another wave knocked them. This time he lost his footing and she slipped from his hold, her lips torn from his, the seal—the flare of insanity—severed.

She staggered and straightened at the same time as he. It wasn't fast, it was confused. And then three feet separated them. Breathless she glanced down and saw her nipples were diamond hard. So were his. So was something else of his.

Shocked she slowly stared up his straining body. He too was breathless and she tried not to stare at the way his gorgeous chest was rising and falling, and his defined abs rippling. Instinctively she lifted her hand to her mouth, automatically moving—too late—to hide the swollen sensitivity of her lips and their blatant, desperate ache for more. Finally she dragged her hungry gaze all the way up and she looked him in the eye.

His expression was burnished with arrogant defiance and his lips were curled into a saturnine smile. 'You more than met me halfway, Maia.'

'I stumbled—'

'You wanted it and you *liked* it.' He turned away.

She didn't like that he turned his back to her. She felt instantly cold.

'Aron,' he said gruffly.

'Your Highness.'

Stunned, Maia swivelled towards the beach. There was an ancient man walking towards them on the fine white sand, impassively holding white towels and studiously not looking her in the eyes.

How long had he been there watching them? The awful thing was she'd been so lost to passion that they could have been in front of a *stadium* full of people staring and she wouldn't have stopped. She wouldn't have given a damn. Because all she'd wanted was more of Niko's touch. That realisation shocked her all over again.

But the elderly manservant didn't bat an eyelid. Apparently he wasn't fazed by a fully clothed, soaking woman being kissed to within an inch of ecstasy in the midday sun.

'Thank you, Aron. This is Maia. Can you please show her around the facilities. I would like her to be accommodated in the coral room.'

'It is already prepared, Your Highness.'

Niko turned to her and an exasperated but amused look entered his eyes. 'Go with Aron, Maia. You'll be perfectly *safe* with him.' He underlined the word edgily, as if mocking her for feeling unsafe with him.

Well, she *wasn't* safe from the very mixed feelings Niko wrought within her. But she didn't move. She refused to jump to his every order in the way he so clearly expected. 'What are you going to do?'

His eyes widened and his already charged body tensed. Yes, he was definitely unused to being questioned. He never had to answer to anyone. But Maia stared at him expectantly and she was determined to wait for an answer.

'Kingly things,' he said stiffly.

'*Kinky* things?' She deliberately misinterpreted what he'd said and allowed tartness to sharpen her tone. 'Well, that makes total sense.'

Yes, it was childish. And yet she was totally satisfied when she saw his jaw drop as she turned her back on him and stalked up the beach.

CHAPTER SIX

NIKO LITERALLY, FIRMLY, rubbed away his rueful smile with his fingers on his lips as he watched Maia march up the beach towards his favourite place on earth. Her stiff spine radiated outrage but even so he couldn't resist appreciating the lush curve of her waist and sensual flare of her hips that he could now finally see because her shapeless clothes were sodden and stuck to her skin. His hand tingled from where he'd gripped her softness only seconds ago. Happily the horrible headscarf had been lost at sea in that frantic swim and her hair had loosened from its knot in all the effort. Now it hung in gleaming black ropes right to the small of her back— the silkiness had whipped his skin when he'd brought her flush against him and he wanted to wind it around his wrists.

As she stalked off like a wilful, dangerous Siren all he wanted was to rip that unsexy outfit from her beautiful body, clutch her close and bury himself deep in her astonishingly fiery hold. Instead he just stared, sluggishly processing what the hell had happened. How had he responded to her touch so ravenously? Why, when once more the way she'd spoken to him had been shocking?

Unvarnished. Honest. Devastating.

'Be gentle and take it slow' had been the unsolicited advice from that damned doctor. Hell. Niko had just ravaged her mouth in full-out beast mode. Explicitly carnal and with extremely uncharacteristic possessiveness, he'd displayed zero finesse nor the patience to seduce her slowly given what he knew about her.

Yet apparently she hadn't needed slow, had she? She'd been as hot as he. Hungrily rubbing those lush breasts against him in a way that made him forget where they were, why they were here and hell, frankly who he even *was*. All that had mattered was capturing the full force of her fire in his arms. Damned if she hadn't burned his brains to ash in an instant. And she hadn't been afraid to throw out an equally inflammatory comment in the aftermath, had she? Though then she'd turned red and fled. That seemed to be a habit of hers. Was she wary of reprisal? Maybe she should be. But maybe one day soon she'd have to face the full consequences of letting her sassy, sweet mouth run amok on him…

But that flush suggested she'd been as surprised by her snap as he was. She was like a skittish kitten testing new-found claws. Maybe it all *was* new to her. Because surely if she'd been like this with any other guy before now, no way would she still be a virgin. Just none. So either she hadn't been playful like this, or some fool had never picked up on her sensual challenging side and encouraged the hell out of it. That aspect of her definitely ought to be developed, and wasn't Niko just the man to help her with that?

No. No, he was not.

Grimly Niko put his rampant lusty thoughts on ice.

This wasn't one of his usual offshore weekend flirtations. This was a permanent problem and the whole thing was complex enough without him tossing gunpowder into the mix. For all his security reports, he barely knew her. More importantly she certainly didn't know him, nor what royal life was like or what the expectations on her would be. He had to keep his focus on the basics required. That was an arrangement they could both cope with. One that would be supportive. Discreet. Manageable. *Controllable*. He'd intended to keep things calm this morning, not to let his annoyance about her escape attempt show. He'd been going to make her feel *safe* and confident about staying in Piri-nu with him. That she had nothing to fear from him.

Instead he'd gotten his hands on her the first chance he had and dived into an all-out lust-fest that had backfired completely—

With a frustrated growl he turned his back on the beach so he couldn't stare after her anymore. He'd return to the boat and ensure the damned thing was moored securely. He hadn't had the chance to double-check what with her rash leap overboard. Plus he'd get the electronic gear he'd not been able to bring in the water. He'd not had the mental capacity to explain all that to her when she'd questioned him on his plans. Truthfully his mental capacity had been zilch. And maybe it was rude of him not to take the time to show her to her room, but if he'd taken her in there now he'd have seduced her in seconds. Given what had just happened in the water he knew he could. He'd have taken everything but frankly, given the battle he was still having with an extremely intense arousal, they'd have finished in less than five minutes.

Not happening. *Ever.*

Because while Niko wasn't afraid of having fun with a woman, he did *not* lose control of himself in any situation. Yet just then he almost had and he *still* couldn't stop thinking about the one tiny taste he'd had of her. She'd been ardent and sweet and the answering thrusts of her tongue as her wet body writhed against his were going to haunt him hard. As it was, all he'd wanted for the last twenty-four hours was to have her in his arms again and it had been hotter than he'd ever imagined, so how was he going to cope with this intense attraction while they were stuck together here?

He needed a bloody ice bath.

Maia had to force herself not to press her hands to her lips, which were still tingling from the intense press of his. She desperately suppressed memories of that teasing flick of his tongue, the sheer force of his passion—the sensual guidance of his hands, of his lips, compelling her to open for him—but her body rebelled, still tingling, still aching for more. Steadying her shaken emotions was impossible so she forced herself to focus on what she could *see*. The problem was that what she saw simply made her already erratic pulse skip even more.

It was pure, undiluted paradise—the beach was a sweeping arch of sand that led to lush emerald trees while a dramatic mountain rose up behind. She tried—and failed—not to fall deeper beneath the spell of her location with every step. If she were alone she might have cried at the beauty of it—the *luxury*—but she wasn't alone so she held it together like always as Aron, the elderly servant, pointed out the facilities in a smooth, calming tone that she deeply appreciated.

The stunning mansion was secreted away in the heart of lush green palm trees, and its own focal point was a gorgeous outdoor area. Aron gracefully gestured to the lounge chairs dotted perfectly at the rear of the infinity-edged salt-water pool and spa and to the dining area with elaborate outdoor kitchen and barbecue. Conscious that she was dripping a trail of water behind her, Maia was speechless as Aron showed her through main building—the relaxing living room, the formal dining room, then large gym and den on the lower floor.

'Your suite is this way.' Aron then led her to a separate building connected to the main via a shaded walkway. 'The king's suite is through there.' Fortunately they kept walking. 'It has his study and other personal facilities.'

The bedroom suite Aron took her to was a dream, with polished wooden floors, vast windows and dreamy, luxury linen. It encapsulated peace and space and everything a tired lonely person could long for. Light, neutral drapes created a soothing frame for the most stunning view she'd ever seen. While she loved the water and was so at home there, this was the best slice of land she'd ever seen. This was pristine beach and beautiful trees and it evoked a sense of serenity as well as that beautiful blue of the water—the endless expanse to the horizon was so evocative of the freedom she'd always longed for.

'Are there other staff on the island?' She finally over-came her embarrassment enough to indulge her curiosity.

'Rarely,' Aron replied.

'None at all?' She was amazed. While she didn't want to be rude, Aron seemed awfully old to have to maintain this entire property all by himself.

'The king values the privacy he has here.' He shook his head. 'I served the king's father and his grandfather before him. It is an honour to work for King Niko and this is the most beautiful place in the world.'

She wondered if this was a reward for the elderly loyal staffer. 'You don't get lonely?'

'Since my wife passed on it brings me peace to be here. My children and grandchildren are frequent visitors. King Niko allows them use of all the facilities. He's very generous.'

She felt that embarrassment heat her cheeks again. 'Does the king often stay here?'

Did he bring other women here? Aron hadn't ap-peared to be phased by that mortifying display on the beach. Perhaps all this was normal for Niko. Yet the thought of other women being here and enjoying this luxury made her unreasonably irritable.

He was frequently photographed with women when he was abroad, but not filmed actually *kissing* any—a hand on the back, perhaps, a gesture that could be con-strued as chivalrous, not lecherous. But the insinua-tion of intimacy was there—the stars in the model or actress or socialite's eyes said it all. Every time. With every one of them. But Maia was not jealous. She had no interest in nor claim on him. Except if they *were* to marry—then that would have to be discussed, because she refused to be an unwanted wife whose husband repeatedly cheated on her. She wasn't going to sit around and be humiliated even if the marriage was to last only a short time.

'He stays only occasionally and for a few nights at most,' Aron answered. 'Please let me know if there is anything you need. This room hasn't been used since the refurbishment and I might have forgotten a couple of things in my hurry to get it ready this morning. Do forgive me if that's the case.'

'When was the refurbishment?' she couldn't resist asking.

'Coming up eight years now.'

'No one has stayed in this room in *eight* years?' Maia gazed again at the serene, spacious room with its stunning view. What a waste it seemed. Yet something curled within her—pleasure at being special—that she was allowed to use this precious space when almost no one ever did.

Of course, it dawned on her only a moment later that if Niko did bring women here they probably stayed in *his* suite. *Idiot.*

'I think you've done a beautiful job preparing the suite. Thank you,' she muttered shyly. 'I'm sorry about this puddle I've left…'

Aron's eyes twinkled. 'King Niko likes things to be very relaxed here and it is a beach house, at heart. A little water won't hurt the floors. I will leave you to freshen up now.'

She didn't know what was to be expected. What they were going to do. How she was ever going to get free now. She was grateful for the space to process what had happened. Of course her escape from the palace had been too easy to be real. Perhaps it was part of a plan to subdue her—to seduce her into submission? If so, how she was going to resist him? Part of her simply didn't want to. Maybe he would try everything he could to get what he wanted. But maybe she would do the same.

She peeled off her damp work trousers and hung them over the railing in the hopes they would dry super quickly in the rising heat as the day matured. She wanted to check out that pool and the beach but she wasn't sure of the protocol. Playing it safe she went to the bathroom and rinsed off in the gorgeous shower—trying not to think about that kiss while constantly thinking about nothing else. When she emerged she discovered her clothes were gone from where she'd hung them. Aron had clearly slipped in and out of her suite again as there was now a silk robe on the small chair at the foot of the massive bed.

She pulled it on, almost able to wrap it around herself three times over, and walked out onto the private deck, breathing in the view. A hammock was strung between two trees down by the beach. Beyond that she saw Niko paddling a small boat back from the fishing boat they'd anchored in the bay. She watched as the waves pushed him onto the shore. He hopped out, splashing in the shallows to pull the boat further up onto the sand. Maia's jaw dropped as he did—not because of his display of skill and strength, but because the man was as naked as the day he'd been born.

She *should* look away. But she didn't. She couldn't. She just stared, her mouth still ajar as he secured the small boat and then splashed back into the sea. Once deep enough he lifted his arms in a graceful arc and dived. His movements were powerful and so assured, she knew he'd swum this cove a million times. This was his home and he'd shed the regal persona and the weight of duty—coming here he was free to be himself. She saw the strength and purpose in his stroke. She also saw the joy. Something within her softened towards him and sent a pulse of desire around her body.

She shouldn't be watching him. It was pure voyeurism but she simply couldn't tear her attention away. Eventually she realised a low throbbing sound was growing louder. An incoming helicopter. Niko must have heard it too because he swam back to shore. He walked out of the water onto the beach. Scooping up a towel that he wrapped around his hips, he stood at the shoreline, his back to her, his face lifted to the sky, watching for the machine.

It didn't land. Instead a large pallet was released on a line. She saw a figure in the open hatch, making some sign to Niko. She saw the wide slash of his smile as he moved to unhook the crate, the movement of his chest as he laughed and made a rude gesture with his hand. The guy in the helicopter made one back. They were friends then. Niko and the scary-looking guard who always wore those reflective sunglasses.

Niko was already unfastening the net securing the crate when Aron emerged from the house wheeling a trolley with him. As the noise from the helicopter faded she could hear their laughter as the Niko stacked the boxes from the crate to the trolley. As he then pulled the trolley towards the house, he glanced up towards her. It was too late to draw back out of sight. She made herself remain still. She wasn't going to apologise for seeing all that she had. If he was going to flaunt himself around the place completely naked, then he was going to be seen.

Five minutes later someone knocked on her door and she was not disappointed to see Aron and not Niko standing there when she opened it.

'Some items have arrived for you, ma'am,' he said. 'The king was aware you had only the clothes you were wearing and hopes you'll find something acceptable in this selection.'

Stunned, Maia stepped back to let Aron wheel the trolley in. There were three large boxes. That was a lot of clothing.

'Would you like assistance to unbox?' he asked politely.

'No, thank you, Aron,' Maia said softly, mortified that she had to be clothed like some urchin. 'I'm sure you've a lot more important things to do with your time. I can manage.' She didn't want to make more work for the man. 'Where would I find the king if I wanted to thank him?'

'I believe he's gone back into the water.' With a slight bow, Aron closed the door behind him.

Maia turned back to the windows. Sure enough Niko was stretching out in the water with those strong, long strokes again. Probably still not wearing anything. Well, she couldn't lose all time again just by standing there staring at him. She faced the boxes. Part of her wanted to reject everything he offered but she hadn't the confidence to emulate his nudist approach. Finally curiosity won and she opened the first box, and it was like every Christmas she'd never had.

As she unfolded each item she placed it in the large walk-in wardrobe. There were bikinis in bright shades, shorts, loose linen trousers and long cool dresses—some floral, some neutral, all soft and beautifully stitched and gorgeous. These were quality items that she could never afford to buy for herself. The shoes were mules and slides, perfect beach wear where it didn't matter if the size wasn't quite right but as it happened they fit perfectly. There was a box of toiletries with moisturiser and after-sun lotion plus a small make-up kit of sampler-sized products that she hadn't the skill to use.

But she used the comb and coiled her hair into a high bun, hot from the effort of unpacking the embarrassment of riches that had been given to her. Worst of all she loved every item.

She stroked the yellow bikini, drawn to the bright colour. Despite having just showered, she would explore that pool and hopefully avoid him for a while yet.

The temperature of the water was just cool enough to be refreshing in the heat of the afternoon and it was luscious. She floated, feeling guilt bloom for her attempted escape this morning. It worsened because part of her was pleased to be brought to this place. She didn't *deserve* to enjoy it given she'd run away and only made things even more difficult. Wincing with embarrassment, she dived deep to escape her own thoughts.

As she surfaced she spotted Niko walking towards her. Fortunately he had a towel around his waist. Maia meant to keep her eyes on the water but she just stared—hot again even while standing chest deep in water.

'How long do you plan to keep me here?' She went on the defensive.

'As long as it takes to figure out what we're going to do.'

'I thought you'd already decided what we're going to do.'

'Perhaps we need longer to talk things through.'

'You mean you've discovered you need longer to get me to agree to whatever you want?'

He watched her.

'Because you're used to making all the rules. Everyone saying yes, all of the time.'

'You think life is ever that simple?'

'Mostly, for you. You're the king.'

He stared down at her for a long moment and she had the odd feeling he was literally counting beats before answering her. 'You haven't actually given us a chance to talk. You assumed you'd have no voice and no choice, so you ran before even trying,' he said calmly. 'And I don't entirely blame you when—'

'You might think you do, but you don't know anything about me,' she interrupted hotly, uncomfortable because he was right.

'Then why don't you talk to me?' he countered. 'Why not give us a chance to get to know each other and work this out *together*?'

She waded to the opposite side of the pool and climbed out. The thought of being bracketed with him made her restless and her immediate instinct was always to run. Yet he sounded so damned reasonable. How was it that now she felt bad for skipping out when he was the one who'd kidnapped her in the first place in a display of power and might, money and control? How did she end up feeling guilty for not 'giving him a chance'?

And how had she been such a fool as to get out when he was standing right beside her towel and now she was stuck in nothing but a tiny bikini?

'We have to work this out, Maia,' he said quietly. 'And contrary to what you seem to think, I don't have all the answers already. Perhaps you do?' His expression tightened as he stared at her. 'I'm looking forward to hearing what you had planned to do once you'd made it to that next island.' He picked up a towel and walked towards her—stretching out his hand to offer it to her.

Utterly awkward, she stretched to take it, trying to maintain as much distance as possible between them.

His gaze was harder now and she heard him draw a sharp breath. 'I'm going to shower and change for dinner. We'll eat in twenty minutes.'

CHAPTER SEVEN

CHANGE FOR DINNER? Maia scrambled as soon as he'd stalked off. He was displeased. Well, that made two of them.

After another quick shower she left her hair loose, it was almost dry already, and pulled one of the dresses on. It was modest yet sensual at the same time because of its silkiness. She walked out to the patio, unsure whether they were dining in the formal dining room or in that outside area.

She licked her lips, pangs of hunger hitting hard. For the first time since her abduction she felt like eating a full meal. But she paused when she spotted him staring at her from across the patio. She just stared back. He wore linen shorts and a barely buttoned shirt that displayed the very fine physique she well knew he had. He'd shaved so that angular jaw was emphasised together with those impossibly stunning cheekbones.

'Some of the clothing fit you okay.' He cleared his throat almost awkwardly. 'One of my men went to your father's boat to collect some of your things but...'

Shame curled upwards, a constant. 'I only had a few work clothes there.'

'That's what he said.'

She studied the large stone tiles she was standing on. It was worse than that. She only had one pair of shoes to her name and the few clothes she owned bore the boat's logo and were old and stained. 'I don't need much. I—'

'Don't,' Niko said gruffly.

She looked up, startled at his tone. He'd silently moved nearer.

'Don't make excuses for him,' he added quietly.

The anger in his eyes torched something within her. He knew. Because his soldier had seen. And she was horrified.

'What did your soldier tell him?' she asked.

'That the king had heard of your work and wanted to try some. That you'd agreed to come to the palace early in the morning and had been so excited you'd forgotten to leave a note.'

Excited. Maia blinked. 'And he believed that?'

'He wanted to know how much you were being paid. My man was at pains to reassure him that you were being very well taken care of in all areas.'

But her father wouldn't have been bothered about *that*. It was only ever about money for him. She curled her hands into fists but knew them to be useless. 'You must think I'm pathetic.'

'No. Why would you—'

'Because I should have run, right?' she interrupted roughly. 'I should have run away from *him*. From *that* life. But I didn't. Not in all these years'

'How could you? You were stuck in the middle of the ocean most of the time. What were you supposed to do? He didn't pay you. He controlled everything. You had no money. No real options.'

'You know everything.' She stared at him in consternation and pressed her fists to her flaming cheeks.

'I know a few sparse facts. I have no idea about the full picture.' He hesitated. 'Maybe you can talk to me about it sometime,' he added quietly. 'Not now. But maybe when you're ready.'

She appreciated the attempt but he was inviting an intimacy neither of them really wanted or were ready for. She saw the guarded look in his eyes and she felt so sorry.

'I needed time,' she explained softly. 'I know we have to work this out. I wasn't intending to run away forever. I was never going to stop you from...' She sighed. 'I just needed to claim some control of my own. I had no idea what I was going to do. I just needed to prove—to myself more than anything—that I could. I can't be a doormat for the rest of my life. I just can't.'

He looked down and cleared his throat. 'I do have something else for you.'

She closed her eyes in instant rejection. She didn't want anything more from him. She didn't want to be this charity case that he felt sorry for. She didn't want to be this *helpless*.

'Maia.'

She opened her eyes and saw his fist right in front of her but then he unfolded his fingers and she saw her whittling knife resting in his palm.

'Oh!' Her heart leapt. 'You have my knife.'

He nodded.

She rapidly blinked. 'You trust me enough to return it to me?'

'I figure it's not going to do too much damage if you turned it on me.'

'Are you sure about that?' She attempted a weak joke to cover her emotion.

'Not going to go too deep. It's like a paring knife, right? Taking only layers.'

'True.' She cleared her throat. 'But there are some points of a body where damage could be done.'

'Oh?'

'Here.' She pointed to his neck and as the joy of getting the knife back circulated, she warmed to the topic, suddenly laughing. 'And of course, damage could be done to more intimate places.'

He cocked his head, surprise flashing in his eyes. 'But Maia.' He suddenly smiled wickedly. 'Why would you risk damaging something that might bring you so much pleasure?'

'That might *what*…?' She stiffened. 'Oh *please*…'

He threw back his head and laughed freely. 'The look on your face…' He laughed harder.

That embarrassment of before burned off in the heat of his amusement. 'You're shameless.'

'Yes,' he admitted happily. 'Because sex shouldn't be shameful. It should be fun. Life's too short not to enjoy it fully.'

Life wasn't only too short, it sometimes wasn't fair either—and some circumstances didn't allow for fun.

'Now I know to search you for the knife before we go to bed.'

'*We're* not going to bed,' she growled.

'Hmmm.' He was so close to her, so close but not quite touching. 'I understand that you know how to protect yourself but you're not going to need those skills with me, Maia. Because I'm not going to do anything that you don't want me to. I won't come near you again unless you ask. Or I ask and you say yes.'

Neither of those things were going to happen.

But the flutter of temptation strengthened every second he smiled at her. She wasn't going to be able to hold it back. 'Your playboy reputation is fully deserved then.'

That smile deepened. 'You don't think it's part of a ploy to keep up the international profile of Piri-nu?'

'Please. A virile playboy king as a promotional strategy? Surely you can think of something better than that.'

'People like romance and possibility.'

'Well, you definitely give them plenty of possibility.'

'Oh so judgemental, my sweet.'

'You don't take anything seriously.'

'No,' he corrected her outrageously. 'I haven't taken any *relationship* seriously. Every few months I enjoy spending time with women who would have no intention of fulfilling a duty that isn't theirs and suppressing their own dreams. Women like that are safe choices for me, Maia, and I'm a safe choice for them. It's fun and I'm not going to apologise for occasionally enjoying myself when I work hard the rest of the time. It's not even that often. Yet you seem to resent that I sometimes blow off steam?'

She was shocked by his blunt honesty. And suddenly jealous. 'Maybe I've worked hard my whole damned life. Maybe I want to blow off steam too and I've just never gotten the chance—' She broke off, embarrassed.

'Never? No chance? No cute guest one time?' He stared at her intensely.

She winced. 'My father's guests aren't exactly my type.' She didn't want to talk about this. Didn't want his pity.

'So you have a type?'

'I haven't had a chance to figure that out yet.'

'Because you've never had the chance to meet anyone else.' He paused thoughtfully. 'It's not fair.'

His humanity was worse.

'I'm sorry,' he added. 'This whole situation really isn't fair.'

Not on *either* of them. She was never the bride he'd ever have selected for himself.

'I guess we can't all get whatever we want, whenever we want. Not without repercussions or some kind of price to pay,' she muttered.

'We should get what we want *sometimes* though. Even just some of what we want,' he countered. 'Just as we can't always get everything we want, we also shouldn't have to miss out on everything all of the time. We ought to be able to get some things sometimes, right?' He regarded her steadily.

'There's still a price. There's always a price.' For people like her anyway.

He looked at the little knife he still had in his hand. 'Perhaps you're right.'

Maia couldn't answer him. The thing she wanted to get? Him. Just him. His attention. His touch. And she was angry with herself for being that predictable. That needy.

'Truce, Maia?' He held the knife out to her.

'Okay.' She took it from him. Maybe she would take all she could from him. 'Truce.'

Niko made himself take another deep breath and counted to five while doing so. Anything to try to keep his focus. But he kept failing. Any calm he might have recaptured through his marathon swim session this afternoon had been instantly tossed overboard at the sight of her in that flowing dress that clung in only a couple of very soft-looking places. As for her stunning hair—it was finally loose and visible to him. She had beautiful jet black tresses that were so long, so rich in fullness and colour that all he wanted was to run his hands the length of them and pull her closer. He wanted to feel its silkiness tease his skin as she straddled him and bent her lush mouth to—

He was meant to be providing reassurance and building trust! Not teasing her about them getting it on, and worse, letting his imagination venture into a heated intimacy that he surely didn't actually want!

But curiosity was in control—he was fascinated by her and desperate to find out more about her. And the realisation that her inexperience wasn't because she wasn't interested but that she'd just never had the chance for fun before was stunning. He'd been an idiot not to understand that already. And he was grateful that she'd not suffered worse at the hands of any of her father's guests. All of whom were greedy and unafraid of skirting the law.

She shifted restlessly. 'We ought to go inside and have dinner.'

She was running away from the intensity between them again. 'So soon?'

'I imagine Aron's gone to a lot of trouble and I don't want to disrespect him by taking so long that his food spoils.'

For a second he was startled. But her consideration made sense. Had that happened to her?

'People who are spoilt sometimes aren't conscious of the effort made around them,' she said.

That was possibly true although not, he preferred to think, of himself though. 'Aron knows me and my timetable here very well. He prepares cold salads because I'm often late to dine here.'

'Because you lose track of time while entertaining?'

He suspected the acidic drop in her tone was based more in jealousy than judgement and he wanted *her* to have some fun. He wanted not just to *see* that, but wanted to make it happen for her.

'Because I'm often working late,' he corrected. 'But if I'm not working I'm off swimming or diving, running or climbing, and no one is here to stop me or to ask other things of me—'

'And do you always do all those things naked?'

He paused, momentarily thrown. 'You saw?' He suddenly laughed as she blushed. 'I do apologise if what you saw offended your sensibilities. When you dived overboard I was still fully dressed. I stripped to my briefs but they're uncomfortable for swimming after a while. So when I went back to secure the boat I opted for full freedom over chafing.'

She didn't answer. She just fidgeted with that knife.

'But right here is the one place where I am free to be as naked as I like,' he said quietly, amused. 'My time is wholly my own and Aron understands that.'

She glanced back up at him and he was shocked to see her expression had turned haunted and suddenly he lost himself in those midnight eyes.

'Why aren't you married already?' she asked softly, almost pleadingly. 'What would you have done with me now if you were married?'

He honestly didn't know. 'Fortunately that *isn't* the case.' And he guessed that was one thing to be grateful for. 'We're both single so the solution is simple for us.'

'But marriage isn't simple for anyone. You shouldn't be forced into something you don't want either.'

'I do want this.'

'No you *don't*.' She shrugged. 'Why has it been so complicated, Niko? What's not "safe" about a serious relationship? Why has it been so impossible to consider settling down?'

'I am trying to settle down now, am I not? *You're* the one being obstructive in that plan.'

'Only because you think you have to. Not because you *want* to. Why don't you ever want to?'

She saw that truth and he realised he'd told her too much. Now he was going to have to tell her more.

'I don't think it's fair to burden someone else with this lifestyle,' he said.

Maia glanced around. 'Yes, so terrible to ask someone to share a Pacific paradise with you. All these awful palm trees and coral reefs and the space to swim and dive, run or climb…' she echoed with a little laugh. 'Naked even. It really is just wicked of you.'

'*This* isn't the daily reality of my life.' He chuckled. 'This is the holiday that I get only occasionally. There are limits on what I can do and I know you're not going to believe me but many choices that other people take for granted get taken away.'

'But you also have many choices that other people may never get. Everyone faces sacrifices and limitations in their lives.'

'It's not the same.' He shook his head. 'Your life isn't your own. You have a duty not just to your family, but to all the citizens of the country, and to the country itself. People want to know you. You're expected to uphold the values. To bring prosperity, to maintain peace, to keep the country progressing at the same time.'

But it sounded weak to him. This was a woman who'd intensely experienced not having a life of her own—just in a wholly different way.

'I get that it's a big job but why do you think someone wouldn't want to share it?' she asked. 'Or support you in it? Do you think no one but you could handle it?'

She thought he was arrogant. That he was making more of it than what there was. She was wrong.

'Because the reality is more exhausting and frankly more mundane. It's not all glamour. There are a lot of meetings. Many decisions. Seven days a week. It's relentless.' He sat back.

He'd seen people's health suffer. More than once.

His mother had struggled, the strain of her emotions weakening her as she strived to please everyone. While his grandmother had suppressed every emotion she ever had and become an automaton—barely a human in the end. And his father? He'd lost the love of his life and then totally self-destructed.

'So you have little flings when you're overseas because there's no threat of someone taking them seriously?' Maia asked.

'If I seduced some local society beauty she would offer to sacrifice everything in her life. Her family would expect it of her and they would expect me to ask it of her. I'm never asking anyone to do that.'

'But isn't that what you're asking of me?' She paused. 'Because of the baby?'

But she didn't have much in her life to sacrifice—he could offer her far more than she'd ever had. He gritted his teeth. 'Not everything. Not necessarily forever.'

'How can it not be?' She stared at him hopelessly. 'I can't ever walk away from my child and I get the feeling you won't do that either.'

'No,' he said huskily. 'But I can give you much that you've never had, Maia.'

She looked up, those deep eyes all mystery. All intensity and pain. And rejection.

'We make a *temporary* fix to ensure this child has all they are owed,' he said roughly. 'We can do that at least, can't we, Maia?'

'I'm not saying yes to anything yet,' she said.

That she hadn't instantly said no was oddly enough for now. He didn't want her polite acquiescence. He wanted her to give him some lip again. He wanted that quite literally.

He inwardly groaned. The sudden single-track groove of his mind and the endless ache to pull her into his arms and kiss her was appalling. But the desire didn't spring from any goal to seduce her into saying yes. But to make her simply feel good. He wanted to give her pleasure.

So much for staying away from her. Yet it seemed she couldn't help reacting to their chemistry either. Which meant they might have to deal with it head-on at some point. It just had to be more thought-out and considered. She needed to understand the boundaries and limits of any relationship they embarked upon. So did he. It would solve several problems. Including the believability of their sudden marriage. Beautiful, warm, yearning, sensual. He'd lost his head for her warmth and innate sensuality...

But she was far more vulnerable than he'd realised and he didn't want this destroying her. He couldn't bear to see that happen again.

At least they'd had some moments of laughter in there. Maybe he could build on that instead.

'I'll just get the food Aron has prepared.' He fetched the small trolley Aron had left in the shade and lifted the silver domes that protected the simple salads. Fresh fish rested on ice.

'I use a table top grill to cook the fish,' he said. 'It's very thinly sliced so it only takes moments. Are you hungry?'

'To be honest I'm starving.'

'I'm sorry, I should have considered that sooner.' He gestured to the table. 'Juice? Sparkling water?'

'You don't want a glass of wine?' she asked.

He shook his head. 'You're not—'

'Don't let that stop you from having any.'

'I can cope without pleasurable indulgences for a while, Maia.'

Her startled gaze shot to him. Yeah, she was definitely thinking along the same lines as he was. All the time.

He'd have a whisky when she'd gone to bed and he could ease the tension in every single muscle. For now he had to just stop bloody staring at her.

'Maybe I'm not the spoilt jerk you want to see me as,' he said.

'You're a little bit spoilt,' she muttered mutinously.

'Yeah, well you're a little bit stubborn.' He sighed. 'Neither of us is perfect, apparently. But we can both try our best, right?'

She nodded.

'I apologise if you were expecting something more Michelin five-star with fancy sauces. We keep things simple here.'

Fresh salads. Fresh caught fish. Fresh sliced fruit.

'Aron seems old to be working still,' she commented as he put the fish on the searingly hot grill.

'Aron suffered great loss in his life,' Niko said quietly. 'He likes to be busy. But a maintenance team comes each week for a day to turn the place over. They leave meals for the week for him too. Chopping a handful of tomatoes and raking a few leaves is the extent of his work, really.'

'You're protective of him.'

'Yes,' Niko said.

'He's worked for you for a long time?'

Aron knew everything. And he was as guilty, as hurt, as Niko was because of what had happened not just to Niko's aunt but his mother as well. Aron had loved them too. He had failed them too. In that Niko and Aron had each other.

Niko sighed. 'He is very loyal. He made a lot of sacrifices.'

Maia lifted a fork to her mouth and tasted a small morsel. Her eyes closed briefly.

'This needs nothing more. It's naturally delicious. Where did you learn to cook fish like this?'

'Here. I learned to catch it and prepare it too.' He stared at her soft lips, watching the tantalising flick of her tongue, absurdly pleased to see her enjoyment.

'You've been coming to this island since you were little?'

Now he was happy to answer her questions and keep his mind out of dangerous waters. 'We came a lot when I was very young. A lot of long weekends.' His mother had rested on that veranda. He'd not realised that she needed the quiet to restore her fragile emotional energy. He'd not understood how much she needed to convalesce that until he was older—when hearing his father chastised yet again by his grandparents. 'Less in my early teens, I was sent overseas to a boarding school.'

'Why overseas?' She looked surprised.

'It was considered a vital part of my education to mingle with other future leaders and nobility. To learn other languages, history, science and the arts of diplomacy.' He'd made a good friend in particular there. 'I got to see a lot of the world and do things that I might not have had the chance to do otherwise. After my mother died it was a help to be busy there. It wasn't long after I finished that my father then died and I became the heir. I needed to learn much from my grandfather so didn't come here.' He dragged in a breath. 'But after *his* death I came here for a short period of mourning.' He'd just needed to be alone for a few days. 'There'd been a storm and much of the building was damaged. Over the next couple of years I refurbished it.'

'You laid the stonework yourself?' she challenged.

'Some of it, yes. I hadn't the skills for the fine details, but I worked as a labourer for the craftsmen whenever I could. This was a project I put everything I could into.'

He'd worked through his grief. His guilt. Pax had lived on-site and worked alongside him as part of his own rehabilitation. So had Aron.

'Because you love it here.'

'Because I *need* it.' He froze, stunned at his emotional outburst.

To admit that he *needed* anything to anyone was unusual for him and he didn't know why he had. He glanced up. She was gazing at him with those mysterious eyes. If he wasn't careful he'd slip into them and never emerge again. But honestly, right now he wouldn't care if he were lost in them for good.

'What else do you need?' she asked huskily.

He lost all power of speech. His body had the answer. Only the one.

Her eyes darkened. Hardened.

'Don't you need a wife who can provide you with all the usual wifely things a king requires?' She licked her lips. 'Like one who provides more than one heir? Don't you need a woman who will provide support at events and then relaxation for you? Someone who can speak all those other languages with you, one who understands diplomatic nuances…?' She angled her head and hit him where it hurt. 'Shouldn't you have a society beauty of noble birth who's been educated in *all* the arts of keeping her king content?'

The woman she described was *exactly* the kind he should have. And the last one he wanted. Emotion bubbled again but she didn't know how close to the edge he was and she didn't stop.

'Wouldn't your parents have wanted to approve of—'

'My parents were a love match,' he interrupted her harshly. 'My father refused to accept the marriage that was arranged for him. My mother was a local girl he'd met as a teen.'

Maia's eyes widened. And yeah, she knew *nothing*.

'They married in secret so they couldn't be stopped. The formal, public ceremony was a cover-up that took place several weeks later.'

They'd been teen sweethearts who'd vowed to do anything for each other. And had.

'Were they happy?'

He paused and went for the truth. 'They loved each other to the end but no, they weren't happy.'

Maia flinched and suddenly he was compelled to hold nothing back.

'It wasn't a fairy tale, Maia. Love wasn't enough for it to work. My mother was unsuited to palace life and family dynamics were difficult. He tried to protect her but she wouldn't let him sacrifice his duty for her. She tried but it wore her out.'

Look after her.

His father had instructed him every time he left to work and Niko and his mother had come here. Because—soft and empathetic—she was worn out easily simply by loving too much.

'My father loved her and she loved him but she couldn't quite be happy there.' Nor had Niko been able to make her happy—he'd not been able to help her, he'd not been able to stop her from driving away that night. All of that hurt and he couldn't forgive himself for any of it. For his aunt's misery. His mother's. And ultimately, for both their deaths. 'She couldn't cope with his parents' disapproval...'

Maia swallowed. 'What happened?'

'She spent as much time here as she could.'

'They lived separately?'

'No, it was occasional escapes. My grandmother was a rigid, stern woman who thought that everyone should be able to meet her very exacting standards. She did her duty and expected everyone else to do theirs too with no question. Obligation to the crown was everything and she couldn't understand why her new daughter-in-law couldn't handle the sacrifices required.'

But his mother had been a woman who tried to champion everyone and who exhausted herself in the process. Wanting to be the best she could. Never accepting that she was already enough. Never taking the breaks that she needed. Working herself around the clock to try to please his grandparents. The high standards that no one could ever possibly meet. She'd ached for their approval. She'd wanted to please everyone. And that was impossible.

Niko wasn't asking any woman to attempt that on his behalf.

'Your grandmother sounds formidable. Was *hers* a love match?'

'She'd been my grandfather's betrothed since they were very young,' he said, letting all the cynicism colour his tone. 'Arranged marriages don't always work well either.'

Maia looked at him. 'No?'

'My grandfather was not faithful. He was not expected to be. Not even by her. She turned a blind eye to certain infractions. To ensure stability I suppose.' He sat back. 'She dove into being the best queen she could be. But she grew inflexible and bitter.'

Both wives had been failed. But nothing was as bad as what had happened to Aunt Lani, his grandfather's firstborn child. She'd been betrayed—unacknowledged. She'd been *used*.

He looked down at the table. It was his family duty to provide heirs to the nation. But arranged marriages could hopefully be managed. He'd wanted to make his the shortest he could, which was why he'd planned to delay getting married for as long as possible. Then he'd marry someone with her own life. A minor royal from another island nation maybe. His counsellor of state had kept him apprised of possibilities and he hadn't exactly been disappointed when a couple on his list of possibilities had married other men. But a love match would be even worse.

'So you don't want to marry at all,' Maia said.

Somehow she'd had him spilling family stuff he'd never spoken of. Like a mysterious nymph, drawing him into lowering his guard. Yet into danger at the same time. All innocence and confusion and fire.

'I've been delaying it for as long as possible.' He nodded. But now he had no choice and he wasn't going to let her try to convince him otherwise. 'Unlike my grandfather I've always been scrupulous in my use of birth control measures. I've never had a possible incident before now.'

Something flickered in her face. Distaste? Jealousy? It pushed him to provoke her more.

'And just so you know, I've never brought a woman here, Maia. It's too personal a place for me.' He leaned towards her. 'You're my first.'

She stared at him and his pulse thudded at the smokiness clouding those mysteriously deep eyes. 'Am I supposed to feel honoured?'

Feeling finally flowed again. Even if it was a dangerous complication, it was better than the numb emptiness of before. He wanted the tantalising heat and the tempting risk of her explosion. So he dared her again with a drawl of pure intentional arrogance. 'Don't you?'

CHAPTER EIGHT

'I'M UNDER no illusions, Niko. You only brought me here because I tried to run away and it's the one place you could bring me that was secure—other than the palace dungeons. And the dungeons wouldn't do in this day and age. Not for someone in my delicate condition. You'd be universally condemned and that wouldn't do for the popular playboy king, would it?' She lifted her chin. 'So *I* am not honoured at all.'

But that this place was too *personal* for him to bring his lovers intrigued her more than she liked. He didn't like to share certain parts of himself with anyone. She wondered why—his parents' troubles, perhaps. It certainly didn't sound like his childhood at the palace had been blissful.

He came here because he needed time and space to himself. Perhaps he was more of an introvert than his charming facade suggested. Perhaps he needed to recharge and refresh here, where he could soak in the sea and stride to the top of the mountain and feel utterly at peace. At home. Hell, naked if he felt so inclined. She totally understood—and it humanised him too, too much.

A tight smile curved his lips but those angles of his mathematically perfect features sharpened. 'It's getting late. You'll want to go to your room and stay there, Maia. There are sea snakes and other biting creatures that hunt here at night.'

'Maybe I'll bite them back.'

He lifted his hand and showed the mark she'd inflicted had all but disappeared. 'You can't even break skin. Stay inside.'

'What are you going to do?'

He stared at her for a long moment. 'You sure you want the answer to that question?'

She stared right back at him. He didn't intimidate her, he *excited* her. And that was the problem—but it was the one she couldn't resist. 'Yes,' she said. 'If I'm to be stuck with you then I expect to know what you're doing, when you're doing it and who you're doing it with.' She pushed back from the table and took a couple of paces towards the pool to expend some of the energy coiling too tightly within her. 'I'm not going to be quietly content and remain in complete ignorance of my husband's assignations.'

His gaze intensified as he looked up at where she stood in the moonlight. 'So you agree that we'll marry then?'

'I've agreed to nothing. Yet.' Something sparked within her. She didn't believe for a second that he would actually hurt her. Quite the opposite. She had the intuition that he could make her feel something unlike anything or anyone else in the world. 'I'm still considering my terms.'

'Your terms?' He watched her. 'What more do you

want?' He shot her a wolfish smile as he listed the bare necessities he'd provided for her. 'You have food, shelter, clothing—'

'Actually, there was one small issue with that delivery.'

'Oh?'

'There was no underwear.'

The way his eyes widened she knew it had been an inadvertent mistake, not a deliberate strategy. '*What?*'

'It's okay.' She smiled blithely at his breathlessness. 'I can use a bikini.'

He blinked.

'But I didn't tonight,' she added.

His gaze tightened. 'Are you telling me you're wearing nothing underneath that flimsy dress?'

'I figured you wouldn't mind if you noticed. I assumed your lovers would be confident, sensual people but you seem to be blushing.' But she was blushing more because he was looking at the dress as if he could tear it away with one movement. Which, to be fair, he probably could.

'Maia.' His bossy king voice emerged. 'Don't provoke me.'

She struggled to keep her gaze on him. 'What do you mean?'

'I mean I'll prove the impact I have on you in the next second if you don't stop trying to make me—' He broke off and suddenly pushed back from the table to stand. 'If you don't want me to retaliate in kind, then I'd advise you to stop right now.'

Maia remained in place as he walked towards her. She wasn't going to run away from him this time. But in truth, every muscle was locked so tight she couldn't have moved even if she'd wanted to.

'Or do you *want* me to retaliate, Maia?' he asked silkily. 'Is that what this is? Because all you have to do is ask. But maybe you can't quite bring yourself to do that yet. So maybe we change the communication. Maybe you just have to say *no*, and I'll stop. But maybe I'm not going to stop until you do.'

She stared up at him in shock as he cupped her jaw and his other hand lightly ran the length of her hair.

He leaned closer. 'Just take, okay? I'll give and you take.'

Was *that* how this was working? But he was right. It was a gift. Lush little kisses. So different to that passionate, out-of-control onslaught in the water this afternoon, but no less powerful. She melted into his strength and he suddenly bent her back, supporting her completely to then kiss her deeply. She moaned, feeling the passion run right through her. But it wasn't enough. She wanted more. So much more that it terrified her.

'Stop,' she muttered desperately. 'I need you to stop.'

He instantly did but even so she pushed him, straightening and turning swiftly away.

'Maia.' He grabbed her arm before she could escape. 'Stop. Speak to me.'

'And say what?' Hurt bubbled up. 'You proved you can make me want you in an instant. Can't you be satisfied with that?'

'That's not—' He drew a harsh breath and suddenly stepped back. 'Go to bed, Maia,' he said huskily. '*Rest*. You need it.'

As if that were ever going to happen now? Her body

was wired. How had that become a conflagration of such heat and passion so quickly?

But he'd walked away so easily. He'd not tried to convince her to continue. Which was good, right?

No. It was irritating.

She went to her suite, glad of the open windows and whirring fans. She was too hot, too irritable, thinking too much to sleep. Besides, the bed was too big. Too still. She'd spent her life on the water, feeling the gentle swell of the sea. Sometimes the rough waves. Always in motion. She'd never once had an actual mattress. She felt stupid but it was too soft. And it made her think of things that weren't going to bring any kind of peace to her over-imaginative mind. With a frustrated sigh she wrapped the silk robe more tightly around herself and went from her veranda to the hammock. She would cool down for a while in the light wind and listen to the waves.

It was an immediate comfort to lightly sway and stare up at the stars that were so familiar to her. She identified the constellations as a form of distraction, calming herself by remembering the generations of way-finders who'd traversed this ocean several times over—moving from island to island and finding freedom and prosperity.

She didn't know how long she'd been out there but she heard footsteps approaching and lay still, hoping he wouldn't see her. Of course she had no such luck.

'It doesn't matter how much you try to shrink yourself down, that robe is gleaming like a pearl in the moonlight.' He expelled a frustrated puff as he leaned over to look her in the eyes. 'What are you *doing* out here?'

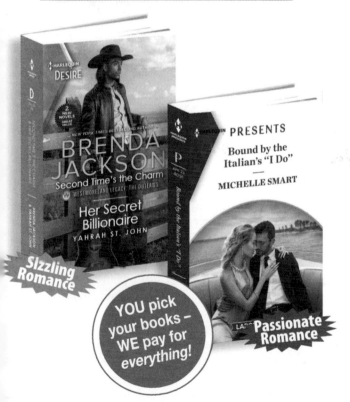

Dear Reader,

Your opinions are important to us. So if you'll participate in our fast and free "One Minute" Survey, YOU can pick up to four wonderful books that WE pay for when you try the Harlequin Reader Service!

As a leading publisher of women's fiction, we'd love to hear from you. That's why we promise to reward you for completing our survey.

IMPORTANT: Please complete the survey and return it. We'll send your Free Books and a Free Mystery Gift right away. And we pay for shipping and handling too! ← *We pay for EVERYTHING!*

Try **Harlequin® Desire** and get 2 books featuring the worlds of the American elite with juicy plot twists, delicious sensuality and intriguing scandal.

Try **Harlequin Presents® Larger-Print** and get 2 books featuring the glamorous lives of royals and billionaires in a world of exotic locations, where passion knows no bounds.

Or TRY BOTH!

Thank you again for participating in our "One Minute" Survey. It really takes just a minute (or less) to complete the survey... and your free books and gift will be well worth it!

If you continue with your subscription, you can look forward to curated monthly shipments of brand-new books from your selected series, always at a discount off the cover price! Plus you can cancel any time. So don't miss out, return your One Minute Survey today to get your Free books.

Pam Powers

"One Minute" Survey

GET YOUR FREE BOOKS AND A FREE GIFT!

✓ Complete this Survey   ✓ Return this survey

1 Do you try to find time to read every day?

☐ YES ☐ NO

2 Do you prefer stories with happy endings?

☐ YES ☐ NO

3 Do you enjoy having books delivered to your home?

☐ YES ☐ NO

4 Do you share your favorite books with friends?

☐ YES ☐ NO

YES! I have completed the above "One Minute" Survey. Please send me my Free Books and a Free Mystery Gift (worth over $20 retail). I understand that I am under no obligation to buy anything, as explained on the back of this card.

☐ **Harlequin Desire®**
225/326 CTI GRTQ

☐ **Harlequin® Presents Larger-Print**
176/376 CTI GRTQ

☐ **BOTH**
225/326 & 176/376 CTI G294

FIRST NAME

LAST NAME

ADDRESS

APT.#

CITY

STATE/PROV.

ZIP/POSTAL CODE

EMAIL ☐ Please check this box if you would like to receive newsletters and promotional emails from Harlequin Enterprises ULC and its affiliates. You can unsubscribe anytime.

HD/HP-1123-OM_123ST

'I'm not used to sleeping in a bed like that.'

'Like what?' He looked so outraged she was forced to explain.

'So big. And flat. And it doesn't move. It's too still.'

He stared at her. 'You sleep in a hammock on board your father's boat?'

'Yes. In the store.'

His jaw went angular.

'I actually like it,' she added hurriedly, seeing the storm grow even bigger in his eyes. 'I prefer it to having my own cabin. It's away from the others and more private.'

'You've lived in that your whole life?'

'I like the sway of it. And I like listening to the waves,' she continued defiantly, ignoring the appalled judgement in his voice. 'The sound calms me.'

He stared at her for interminable seconds. 'It calms me too,' he said brusquely.

To her astonishment he turned on the spot and left her in a jumble of want and misery and confusion. She pressed hands to her hot cheeks. She was hopelessly attracted to him and she had no idea how to handle it. Ten minutes later she heard heavy footsteps again. They were deliberately heavy—because she knew too well how silently he could move when he wanted to.

'I've put up another hammock on your veranda,' he informed her with a growling edge. 'At least there you'll be sheltered from wind and rain. You can bring down the hatches if you want for additional privacy but as it is now no one will see you other than me. There are some blankets and a pillow too.'

'Niko—'

'I have an outdoor shower area in the garden by my suite,' he interrupted her gruffly. 'So don't go wandering if you don't want to see any more…things.'

With that zinger he stomped off again. Maia lay for another moment purely to catch her breath. Then she went back to her own veranda. He'd left a lantern on and she saw the hammock was one of those silk ones more suited to balmy nights than wild weather. Sure enough there was a pillow, a soft blanket inside. He'd even put a table within reach for that lantern with a glass and a jug of iced water as well. He'd thought of everything.

She clambered in and closed her eyes. But she could hear the flow of running water in the distance and knew he was beneath that shower and her mind decided to torment her with a play-by-play replay of him wading deep into the water in all his naked glory…

And how was she ever supposed to go to sleep *now*?

To her astonishment she did sleep—for hours. Even more amazingly she woke not just feeling refreshed but with an odd amount of energy—more alive than she'd felt in weeks.

She went to the kitchen to ask Aron if there was anything she could do but he wasn't there. She waited, unable to resist peeking into the pantry. And when he didn't show after a while she decided to make herself something delicious. That was one craving she could satisfy for herself. She lost track of time entirely and when Niko walked in and skidded to a halt she startled.

'What are you doing?' he demanded. 'I thought you were sleeping in…'

She whirled, putting her knife and block into the

pocket of the apron she'd commandeered. 'I was. Then I woke up.'

'Why are you baking? You don't need to do that here.' He flared angrily. 'I would have gotten Aron to get you some pastry if I'd known you wanted—'

'I know, but I wanted to make them myself.'

'You wanted to stand sweating in the kitchen?' he said sarcastically.

'I felt like doing something. It's not a chore when I *choose* to do it. I didn't think Aron would mind.' She was suddenly worried. 'Will he mind? I haven't seen him at all this morning.'

'Because he's gone to visit his family offshore. We're completely alone here for the next couple of days.'

She stilled. 'Why have you done that?'

'Why do you think I've done that?'

She swallowed and ducked from his gaze.

'But the last thing I want is for you to slave in the kitchen for hours.'

'Well, what am I supposed to do? I can't just sit around…'

'Sit around what?' he prompted.

Staring at him all day. She *needed* distraction. Desperately.

He suddenly smiled. 'You should take the time for yourself, Maia.'

For herself? She wanted him to distract her. 'You don't need to feel sorry for me, Niko,' she flared. 'I don't want your pity. You don't need to spoil me.'

'Why not?' he countered. 'Why shouldn't I feel sorry for you? Why shouldn't I want to spoil you?'

'I'm pregnant. Not useless.'

'I'm not talking about resting just because of the baby,' he muttered. 'Why is it so hard for you to accept a little pampering in your life?'

'I don't need it.'

'Don't you? Doesn't everyone? I sure as hell do.'

Her eyes widened.

'I make no apology for taking breaks. For doing the things I enjoy.'

'Women.'

'Being in the water,' he corrected and then shook his head with a rueful smile. 'You really have a one-track mind, Maia Flynn.'

She felt that heat and suddenly nodded. 'It's a recent thing,' she admitted apologetically. 'Do you think it's the hormones?'

'Maybe.' He leaned against the counter and laughed. 'I'm talking about taking time for myself. Yes, to come here and swim naked all damned day if I want. I like it. Why shouldn't you do whatever brings you joy too? You've worked your whole life. You should be able to have a few moments of peace for yourself.'

'Why can't you believe that I actually was?' She pulled her knife from her pocket. 'I do have a few things like that.'

He was instantly alert. 'Show me?'

For once it was an actual request, not a demand.

'It's just little.' Embarrassed, she pulled the block from her pocket. 'I raided the woodpile, sorry.'

'You can take anything you want.' He studied the partial figurine she'd been whittling. 'You're an artist.'

'Hardly,' she scoffed. 'I'm a hobbyist. It's just something to fill in time.'

'It's more than that.' He held the half-carved minia-ture sea turtle in the palm of his hand. 'Did someone teach you?'

She nodded. 'Our chef, Stefan. He taught me how to make pastry and he also taught me to whittle. Some-times there weren't any offcuts or driftwood or any-thing so we'd just use vegetables. Or coconut shells. Whatever was at hand.'

'You were friends?'

Stefan had been more of a father figure to her than her own father. He'd certainly been more kind. 'His marriage had broken down and he'd lost contact with his own children. I think perhaps with me he had a chance to…' She shrugged. 'He was a good man who'd made some mistakes in the past. He had regrets, you know? He taught me lots of useful stuff—placing orders in each port, haggling in the market, where to find good books in the hostels, diving for shellfish. He helped me with my correspondence school work. I was a distrac-tion for him I guess.'

'I'm sure you were more to him than just a distrac-tion.' Niko glanced into the distance. 'Where is he now?'

Maia plucked the little carving from Niko's palm and put it back in the apron pocket. 'My father can be dif-ficult. He drinks, he's controlling, he's constantly try-ing to make money, but he's not usually violent. When I was a kid Stefan kept me busy in the galley—out of the way and safe—and he introduced me to something I grew passionate about and that I became good at.' She looked at Niko. 'And that was the problem. I got too good.' She smiled sadly. 'I actually thought Dad might say well done, you know? But all he did was terminate Stefan's contract because I could make croissants just as well as him—which wasn't actually true, by the way. But I'd made him redundant and I had to take over the galley full-time.'

Niko's smile had gone—he was all cheekbones of perfection. 'How old were you?'

'Sixteen.'

'How long had Stefan been with you?'

'Since I was two.' Fourteen *years*. She'd lost her best friend overnight. 'I've not had contact with him since he's left.' She turned back to the pastry that had rested long enough. 'I'm sure he's fine. He would have picked up work easily, he was very talented. I don't know why he put up with my father for as long as he did.'

But she felt heartsick about it. If it hadn't been for her he would still have had that job.

'It wasn't your fault, Maia. Your father took advantage of you both and Stefan would have known that. Maybe you're why he stayed as long as he did.'

She blinked rapidly. 'It's in the past.'

'Doesn't mean it doesn't still hurt, sometimes.'

She glanced at him—his own pain hurt him too.

'That's his knife, right?' Niko asked huskily. 'That's why it's your favourite. It's old. It's been well cared for.'

She nodded. He'd given it to her the day he'd had to leave.

The atmosphere thickened with tension. She felt her emotional control slipping. She did not cry. And she wasn't going to now.

'I need to get this into the oven.' She fussed over the pastry dough that had barely rested long enough.

'Of course.' He cleared his throat. 'I'm going to do some work.'

An hour later Maia finished cleaning up in the kitchen. She tore a piece of fresh croissant but it didn't satisfy the hunger gnawing her insides. Hot and restless she went to her room and changed into the yellow bikini and released her hair. But at the pool she found Niko already in there. He'd been floating on his back but when she walked out he splashed and stood, watching her approach. He didn't smile. He didn't speak.

Somewhat intimidated, Maia glanced around in case she'd missed something but the only thing new was paperwork on the table nearest the water. Well, she wasn't interested in reading any of his private royal documents or anything. She turned back and caught his attention roving over her body. She should've wrapped her towel around herself. His frown deepened the nearer she got to the water.

'What's wrong?' she asked.

'Might be best if you run away again, Maia.'

She stopped at the edge of the pool. 'Why?'

A muttered growl beneath his breath. 'Because I am *trying* to behave but I need some space from you in order to get myself back under control.'

'Space from me?' She glanced down.

He rolled his eyes. 'Yes, Maia. From you. From you and your midnight eyes and bountiful breasts and stunning hair that smells so delicious.'

She gaped, feeling her body respond to the astonishing compliments. But she didn't believe him. 'You're struggling with the loss of your lifestyle.'

His eyebrows shot up.

'It's okay.' She paddled her toe in the water. 'I'm actually *not* judging. I get it. You're young and fit. You weren't ready to settle down and you were living life and having fun. So you're used to indulging your appetite and of course it's going to take some…processing that you now can't.'

'I can't?' he echoed blandly. 'Is that what it is?' He waded closer to her. '*You're* young and fit. But you're *not* living life and having fun. You've *never* indulged your appetite and don't try to tell me you don't have one.'

Her smile twisted. 'I'm not a king though, am I?'

'Are you saying people are only interested in being with me because of my status?'

She laughed. 'Sure. Yeah. That's definitely it.'

He shook his head. 'You can't think of any other reasons why they might want to be with me?'

She shook her head.

'No?' He rested his hands on the edge of the pool and looked up at her, laughter in his smouldering eyes. 'Not any? Cutting me down to size again, Maia?'

'It's impossible. You're too arrogant,' she muttered.

'I might be arrogant, Maia. But I also know when a woman is interested in being with me.'

Her pulse skittered and she stiffened her decidedly shaky legs.

'She might look at me a little too long. Especially when she thinks I'm not watching her. But I am. Because I'm acutely aware of her too. And I'm attuned to her responses.' He levered out of the pool and walked towards her. 'I watch her breathing. Her blush. The beat of her heart. The look in her eyes. So many snippets reveal secrets.'

Maia couldn't move. She also couldn't stop trembling. 'Maybe she's got a fever.'

'Oh, she surely does. The same one as me. Lust is a fever that steals other appetites and becomes the sole focus until it is all you can think about, all of the time.'

'Must make life quite challenging.'

'Unchecked, it absolutely can. It can make concentrating on other things difficult. Which is why it's good to indulge it before it balloons that far out of control.'

'Is that what happens?'

'I don't know. I've never not indulged it. Whereas you never have. So you tell me.'

She felt an odd dizziness sweep over her and a forlorn wish burst from her. 'Don't laugh at me.'

'I'm not.' He looked into her eyes with a frown. 'I would never laugh *at* you, Maia.'

She wanted to believe that about him. But she wasn't sure. She'd heard the laughter of men from overhead so many times. She'd heard the crew joke about no one wanting her. About how easy it would be to seduce her because she was so starved of attention. She'd heard that exact plan from one younger group of guests. So she'd known to resist the fool who'd come downstairs to deliberately flatter her. The assumption she'd be easy pickings.

'Well, don't flatter me to try to get me into bed,' she added distantly. 'I know guys do that.'

He leaned closer. 'They do?'

She nodded angrily. She'd hid her hair beneath a scarf not only to keep it from getting in her face when in the galley. She'd kept her head down and her body shrouded in a large apron even in the heat to hide. Self-preservation. Avoidance. Even when the cute young guys came on board because they sometimes turned out to be less cute and more pushy.

'I'm not experienced. I'm lonely. I'm unattractive. Because I'm always working hard with no one paying nice attention to me. Meeting almost no one. So hit me with a few generic compliments and I'll be an easy lay, right? It won't take anything much to make someone like me feel special.'

He'd frozen. 'Someone said that?'

'I *heard* them making the plan. They didn't know I could hear everything when I was cleaning their stupid cabins.' She scoffed at herself softly. 'And the tragic thing was I'd thought he was actually quite cute.'

'Maia—'

'So I'm not going anywhere because I'm quite sure you can control yourself,' she snapped at his sympathy. 'But if you can't, *you* can leave.'

He stared at her. 'I'm not going anywhere.'

CHAPTER NINE

THE AWFUL, awful thing was she was shaking and he wasn't even touching her. She quickly turned her back on the pool. The view beyond was incredible but she barely saw it because a wall of heat rose within her and it was unstoppable.

'Maia?'

She heard a muttered oath and his hand felt light on her face. 'You're too hot,' he growled. 'You overdid it.'

He pushed her, leading her to the shallow steps of the pool that were currently in the shade. He made her sit so now the water lapped over her feet.

He moved out of her sightline for a moment. Next minute he pressed a cold glass into her hand. 'I knew you shouldn't have spent hours in a hot kitchen.'

She sipped the juice, savouring the sweet yet acid bite of the pineapple. 'It's not that.'

'No?' He took the drink and drained the remainder before setting the glass on the marble tile beside them. 'Then what?'

She shivered and he sat one step up behind her, drawing her back against his chest. 'Lean on me for a minute.'

His strong legs stretched out either side of her. Encircling her. Reminding her of those moments when he'd held her through that boat journey when she'd been blindfolded. When she'd not known who he was. When she'd not even known she was pregnant. When she'd felt absurdly, yet completely, safe. The safest she'd felt in so very long. Now he ran his hands down her hair, sweeping it from her shoulder, exposing her neck—cooling it. Her breathing slowed.

'Better?' A soft query right beside her ear.

She nodded, unable to resist sinking more fully against him and inclining her head so more of her neck was exposed to the delicious, tickling tease of his warm breath on her sensitive skin. He slid his arms around her waist and, giving up her resistance completely, she rested her head on his chest.

'What do you need, Maia?'

She shook her head imperceptibly. Something she shouldn't.

'Maia?'

A question. An admonishment. A prayer. He was so very gentle and she so warm. Yet goose bumps rose on her skin. Being this close to him filled her with the sweetest, sharpest longing. Every cell yearned for contact with him.

'I cannot resist you,' he muttered.

'But you want to.'

'Because it's what's…honourable.'

'Is it honourable to refuse a woman—' She broke off on a sigh as his fingertips glided to her breast.

'Is that what I would be doing?' he asked. 'Then I won't refuse you.'

Her bikini top slipped down so easily—exposing her

breasts to the air and her nipples to his hands—to the teasing swirls of his fingertips, to a pinch and a soothing stroke. To his palms as he cupped her. She moaned at the press of his mouth on her neck. He kissed, licked, sucked...*savouring*. And she just heated. Melted.

'You never wanted me before,' she muttered sadly.

His laughter was soft. 'I never met you before.'

'You said this happening was extremely unlikely.'

'I was being rude because at that time I was feeling extremely provoked.' He pressed another kiss on the side of her neck. 'I'm never going to be sorry for this, Maia. Will you be? Because if so, we need to stop now.'

'Don't stop.'

He stroked down her belly with a gentle hand that she couldn't resist. Her breath caught as he hit the band of her bikini bottoms. He had one hand between her legs now but not beneath the stretchy fabric of her bikini bottoms. She whimpered, wanting his touch, aching for him to explore her even more intimately. To be in her. Instead those fingers simply teased. Skating over where she was most sensitive. Where deep inside she was slick and soft for him. Her moans escaped, louder, and she moved restlessly, instinctively seeking more. In the drowsy heat of the afternoon she had to close her eyes and somehow he knew. His hold on her tightened and he encased her in a velvety heat.

'No one but me can see you. No one but me can hear you. There's only us.' The possessive satisfaction in his whisper turned her on even more. 'Trust me, Maia.'

She spread her hands wide on his thighs, savouring the tense muscles beneath, the sensual pleasure of pressing them so he closed his hold more tightly around her.

This was what she liked. Being cocooned by him. Not just embraced. But overwhelmed. Overpowered. And yet, she felt such freedom in his hold.

'Let go, Maia,' he commanded. 'I've got you.'

But his hands coaxed. They were so gentle, so relentlessly, devastatingly, frustratingly gentle. She tensed as every muscle locked—strung out in the agony of arousal she was so, so close to breaking.

'Now, darling.' A gravelly whisper.

Her cry was rough and raw as she shuddered and her hands curled like claws into his strong thighs. He pressed them closer still. He was literally her vise. Holding her even as he shattered her. And in the long tumultuous shudders of ecstasy he held her closer still.

Niko wasn't living the rest of his life without touching Maia the way she wanted to be touched. He wasn't saying no to her. *Ever.* He wanted her and he would have her regardless of any damned consequences. Because she wanted him too. He believed in honesty. In taking the good things where and when they could be found. Because life was full of difficulties. For everyone.

'There's nothing wrong with pleasure, Maia,' he said quietly when she'd stilled in his arms and had been silent for a little too long for his comfort.

'I know.' She twisted her head to look at him and there was strength and quiet dignity in her gaze. 'I haven't had it. Not nearly enough of *any* kind of pleasure and honestly, none sexually. Not like that. But I want more. Can you deliver?'

His heart stopped. 'I'll do my best.' But for once his confidence faltered and confusion rose. 'We just need to burn this out,' he said huskily, trying to reassure himself as much as her. 'It's a distraction. We get through it and move forward. Then we can think again.'

She gazed into his eyes, her own slightly dazed. 'It's like that for you too?'

'Yes.' Hell, yes. A round-the-clock fascination from the moment he'd first seen her. But he had to normalise it—minimise it. 'This is chemistry Maia. You've not felt this before?'

She shook her head.

Oh hell. He was screwed. 'It's lust,' he added hoarsely. 'Raw attraction. Nothing more.'

'I didn't think it was anything more,' she growled back at him. 'I don't even particularly like you. You're an autocrat who's completely spoilt and who thinks he can get away with anything.'

He suddenly laughed, deeply aroused. 'And you're a wilful woman determined to get her own way. Neither of us is willing to compromise.'

'It seems not.'

'It's going to be a battle.' And he was going to relish it.

'I don't want to fight. I want you to teach me.'

'Teach you what?'

'How to please you the way you just pleased me.'

He was dumbstruck. His mouth was dry and full of cotton wool or something. So was his brain. Maybe it was the sun but he'd never felt as hot in his life. He kissed her. Couldn't touch enough of her. Couldn't get to everything he wanted. Not soon enough. Not now.

'Teach me,' she breathed again when he released her lips long enough for her to actually speak.

'Just touch me.'

And she did. But too lightly. Not far enough. Not fast enough.

Her hand skimmed over his stomach. 'How many hours do you spend in the gym to keep your body so beautiful?'

'Aren't you glad I do?' he challenged softly, hearing the acidic edge to her question. 'It's turning you on right now.'

Earlier her judgement had scoured—an abrasion he wanted to reject—sliding beneath his armour. But she wanted him not in spite of it but because of it. She liked challenging him on this level. A sensual game in which she wanted to best him. And he would play with her.

'Touch any part of me you want, Maia.' He lay back on the marble, feeling the sun-warmed stone warm his already hot skin. '*Every* part.'

That silenced her. Her eyes went round and suddenly he felt a qualm. Maybe she *would* best him. He watched the sensual ripple of her body—the pure physical expression of arousal as she braved up and straddled him.

He could only stare. She had such beauty—complex, earthy, unexpected. Her newly unleashed sexuality undid him. He couldn't resist cupping her breasts. Wanting to pleasure her again but wary of pushing for too much, too soon. The flush in her cheeks deepened. He saw that spark again. That challenge.

'Don't try to control this,' she whispered. 'Let me be free.'

He almost swallowed his tongue. He lifted his hands from her in surrender. Allowing her to access any bit of him she wanted. He really hoped she wanted that bit currently acting like a damned flagpole. Dazed, he watched the undulation of her hips as she bent above him and explored him with her hands. Her hair teased him and she traced his tattoos with her fingertips, with her tongue, and he breathed in the uninhibited, natural dance of her desire. This absolute release of self-consciousness, of control was a rare gift. He saw the focused gleam in her eyes and was transfixed, suddenly harder than he'd ever been. He was literally aching for her touch and scared to even move in case she pulled away. His mouth was dry but he was unable to swallow. And the sweetness of her sudden, swift kiss did nothing to sate him. He wanted more. He wanted all of her. He felt the need so desperately in a part so deep he'd not even realised it existed.

Five minutes ago her hands desperately rubbing his thighs had driven him to distraction. Feeling the passion, the fervour in her fevered caresses and her aching need had stunned him. There was such heat there, such longing, so much that she'd hidden from him—from the world—for so long. He wanted to draw her out. He wanted her to be free. But his customary eloquence was gone. His customary control gone.

'Maia.' He was hoarse with want.

He *needed* her to touch him. He needed that soft hand right where he was so hard it hurt. He tensed as she trailed her fingers ever so slowly to the waistband of his board shorts. He gritted his teeth, shaking as she slipped her fingers beneath. And then—he who had infinite experience—suddenly, completely lost everything at first contact.

A guttural roar of pleasure and frustration escaped

him as he was tossed into a paroxysm of white-hot ecstasy. He growled again, pumping up into her firm hold,
his pleasure spilling far, far too soon. And what pleasure it was—his whole body, even the damned soles of
his feet, tingled and he gasped for recovery. He'd been
unable to withstand the slightest touch. She'd defeated
him with little more than a sigh and a sweet kiss and a
tentative tug. He stared up at her, stunned. He'd come
at first stroke, mortifyingly quickly, as if *he* were the
virgin, barely coping with a singular caress.

She sat back and doubt entered her eyes. 'Is that it?'

He groaned again and then could only laugh helplessly even as he panted, pressing the back of his hands
hard on his eyes to try to recover his brain. But she'd
utterly overwhelmed him.

'Did I do something wrong?' She sounded shy. 'I
didn't expect it to be so quick.'

'Neither did I.' He laughed again. But then he
dragged in a breath and his energy surged back. He sat
up and wrapped his arms around her so she couldn't
slip from his lap. 'You didn't do anything wrong. That
was just…'

'Just?' She was watching him like a wary little
mouse. All wide eyes and silence.

'Incredible.' He kissed her, then breathed deep again
and stood—lifting her with him—loving the way she
automatically wrapped her arms around his neck. 'If
we stay out here we'll get sunstroke. We need a bed.'

And he needed to get his head together.

But he could only stare at her for a second—clad
only in those bikini briefs, her luscious breasts bounc-
ing with their stiff little nipples rubbing against his

chest like the little lick-me beacons they were… Yeah, she was a wet dream and he did not deserve this. But he refused to be a better man. He awkwardly snagged a couple of croissants from the kitchen counter on the way through to his bedroom. He put her on the bed and handed her one of the croissants before biting into the other. And moaned. Buttery soft and delicious. Of course it bloody was.

And she just smiled at him cheekily. 'Niko?'

Maia was *pretty* sure she'd pleased him. But his groan had seemed awfully sudden and for a second after when he'd looked at her—he'd seemed shocked.

'Eat,' he ordered gruffly.

'I'm fine.'

'Just eat something,' he advised. 'You're going to need it.'

She almost baulked at the ferocious intensity smoking in his gaze. Heat sparked. She was already too aware of the intimate ache deep inside, the hunger barely at bay. Sensation curled through her, making her restless. Heating and slicking deep in secret parts.

He finished his pastry in two more bites and his wicked smile slowly widened. 'You decimate my expectations every time,' he said. 'I should have known.'

'Is that a good thing?'

'I have a feeling we're about to find out.' He frowned at the pastry still in her hand. 'Do I need to feed it to you myself?'

She was astonishingly aroused at the thought.

His eyes sparkled. 'Oh Maia, we're going to have fun together.'

'That is the plan,' she said, desperately nibbling the

edge of the croissant as if she had any control over herself anymore.

Sleeping with him was most likely going to be the biggest mistake of her life. But it was one worth making. She wanted this. To know. To understand. To have him in her arms. Enjoying her and giving her the things she'd been denied so long. Attention. Lust. Ecstasy. The delights of sensuality were a side of life she'd shut away for so long. She wanted what other people had and he could give it to her. He already had. It's just that she was greedy and wanted more. And it was so nice not thinking about anything more. Not worrying about the future. There was only this delicious excitement and that she felt no self-consciousness at all amazed her. She felt utterly safe with him here like this—to say what she wanted, to do what she wanted.

'You're so beautiful.' He pushed her back onto the bed and knelt over her.

She *almost* believed him this time. And then it didn't matter because he was touching her. Stripping the bikini briefs from her. Kissing her. Tasting her. Every writhing inch. Until at last his hands stroked her nipples while his tongue slid over the secret nub of her sex. Her hands stretched wide on the big bed seeking something to hang on to as she shook with ecstasy almost as quickly as he'd done before. But then he still didn't lie with her the way she wanted him to. He got off the bed.

'Where are you going?' she demanded, ferociously angry. Hungry.

She had what she wanted but she wanted more.

His smile was strained. 'I've never been intimate without protection. I'll just get—'

'I'm already pregnant,' she interrupted. 'I know you won't do me or the baby harm.' She lifted her chin and blurted the truth. 'I don't want anything between us. I don't care. I know—'

She broke off at the smouldering intensity as he suddenly swore pithily.

'Are you sure about all this?' He growled. 'It can't be undone, Maia.'

'I'm not stupid—'

'I know,' he bit back. His hands on his hips, a picture of aroused, edgy male. 'But this will change things.'

'Don't feel you have to—'

'*Stop.*' In less than a second he was back on the bed, straddling her, his big hands taking her wrists. 'Stop doubting how much I want *you.*'

She stared up at him. Her lips felt full, her whole body was humming with the remnants of bliss but with an emptiness that ached like nothing else.

Don't take this too seriously.

This wasn't forever. This was dealing with the chemistry neither of them had anticipated. He kissed her and she moaned. Desperate relief. Desolate yearning. The paradox of having but still wanting. Of not wanting it to be over yet wanting it all *now.* She twisted, unable to contain the battle within.

'Maia.' He sealed over her. Pinning her down until she stilled.

She felt him draw in a deep shuddering breath and then any last little doubt was obliterated in the steamy passion of his next kiss. She could kiss him for all eternity. Lose all time, all sense of self.

He lifted her slightly, pushing her legs further apart with his. 'You're going to be mine, Maia.'

She shook her head and swept her hands over his shoulders, feeling the muscles working in his upper back. 'No. You're mine. Just for now.'

He smiled and slid his hand between her legs, guiding the way for the part she really wanted.

She gasped at his ultimate, absolute thrust of possession.

'Maia?' A guttural groan. 'Am I hurting you?' He asked hoarsely. 'I *really* don't want to hurt you.'

'I'm okay.'

'Not the answer I wanted.' His eyebrows flickered and his smile became strained as he ever-so-gently rocked within her.

But the moment of pain had passed and she drew a breath of pure erotic understanding. He was here. Hers. Caressing her from the very inside.

'I like it,' she breathed huskily. *I like it. I like it. I like it.*

He hauled her closer and she liked that even more, barely aware she was moaning exactly that. He surged a little harder, pushing them both closer to an edge from which were was no return. She understood and indulged the primal need to meet him. To rise. Her body hummed, dancing to the beat he set for her.

'Hell, Maia.' A throaty growl of encouragement and approval beneath which she heard his need sharpen.

'Mmmmm?' She arched higher, harder.

A low, sexy gust of laughter made her smile in response. And he kissed her for it. That this could feel so good stunned her. So, *so* good—that just like that he tossed her into that place of heat and blinding, blinding light.

The place she now liked best of all.

Five minutes later she still hadn't the energy to move but it was the most delightful exhaustion of her life. Warm bliss literally shimmered through her veins and every cell was smiling.

'You're okay?' He was so very gentle.

She couldn't wipe the smile from her face either. 'Hmmm. I think so.'

He laughed again, the ultimate smug sound. 'Have I *finally* pleased you, Maia?'

She thought about it for a moment, watched the gleam darken in his eyes and saw the lift to the edge of his mouth.

'Honestly?' She smiled at him with a teasing rush of freedom. 'No. Not yet.'

CHAPTER TEN

DESPITE HER EXHAUSTION, sleep eluded her. Her mind buzzed—unable to process everything. What she'd done. What he'd done. How it had felt. Everything was new. She'd never actually *slept* with someone before and barely slept in an actual bed let alone one as vast as this. She faced one way. Then rolled. Flipped onto her stomach. Rolled again.

'Maia?' His amusement was annoyingly audible.

'How do people do this?' She sighed irritably. After twenty minutes of trying she decided it was impossible. 'I'm going to the hammock.'

'Just hang on, Ms Impatience.' Niko flicked a couple of buttons and cool air circulated more strongly in the room. 'It's just that you're feeling overly sensitised.'

She was about to argue when he pulled her back against him, pressing her close so she was burrowed right into the curve of his body. He slung a heavy leg over hers and wrapped his arms right around her so she was tightly caged in his embrace. It would take a lot to wriggle free. He was like her personal weighted blanket—not just cocooning her, but anchoring her. It was absolute bliss. Her breathing settled. Even if she didn't sleep it didn't matter because she didn't think she'd ever felt as content as she did right now.

'Better?' he asked.

She nodded quietly. Not wanting to break the magic of his hold on her with even a word.

Ten hours later Niko was all but climbing out of his skin waiting for her to wake. He'd peeked in on her three times in the last twenty minutes and she'd been a picture of serenity, her glorious tresses smothering the pillow, her curves peeping from the sheet he'd covered her with. He was pleased she was resting well. Her pulse had picked up after they'd finished last night. He'd known it was a sort of over-stimulated anxiety, he'd felt something similar and the only thing he'd thought to do was simply hang on to her, like a life raft, as the inner storm passed. And it had for them both as she'd finally, fully relaxed in his arms.

He poured his second coffee of the day and rolled his shoulders, easing the tension building in there. She'd stunned him, beautiful Maia, with her uninhibited enjoyment of his touch. He just wanted more. Now.

Finally she appeared, wrapped in a silk robe like a present, and shot him a shy smile. 'I slept in.'

'In a bed and everything, well done.'

She shook her head. 'No need to mock.'

He grinned and got the glass of pineapple juice from the fridge that he'd poured in readiness over an hour ago. He watched her drink it and then edged a croissant towards her.

'Thank you.' Her eyes softened.

She was too easy to please.

Him? Not so much. 'Need anything else?' he asked huskily.

She stared up at him, her midnight gaze mysterious, assessing. After a moment she set the half-eaten croissant down.

'Yes,' she breathed. 'You.'

He hoisted her onto the counter and was buried deep in seconds because she was hot and ready and her uninhibited sighs only encouraged him to go faster, harder. He growled, relishing her energy, and then picked her up and took her back to his bed where she belonged.

But hours later he sighed regretfully and disentangled his limbs from hers. 'I need to do some work. It shouldn't take long.'

'Go right ahead,' she said airily. 'I don't need you to entertain me.'

'Really?' he turned and mocked, tugging her close just because he could. 'You don't need me to help you pass the time in a pleasurable way?'

He didn't like to be so summarily dismissed. But the hitch in her breathing gave her away.

It wasn't until the late afternoon that he finally managed to attempt paperwork. She whittled in the shade and he couldn't stop himself watching her. He made it through about ten minutes before tossing the papers to the side and taking her to the pool to lose himself again in their sensual tangle.

He couldn't get enough of her innate playfulness and spirited tease. There was such a lack of deference in her eyes. He relished her frank enjoyment. That she was his match in this was shockingly unexpected. But then she'd not had it before, had she—pleasure. Not much at all of any kind. It was one thing he could give her. Again and again and again until they were finally through it for good. Then they'd be at peace and could parent this child in a simple, rational arrangement.

'How long does it take to get to the top of the hill?' she asked the next morning.

'Too long for you today,' he said. 'We'd need to take supplies.'

'But are there waterfalls?'

'There are and you can explore them another time when you're more…'

'More what?' She faced him. 'I'm not weak. Niko. I get bad period pain. I thought I might struggle to get pregnant. Apparently that's not the case. Yes, I have some bad moments. But most of the time I'm perfectly fine.'

'You get faint,' he pointed out.

'Land legs,' she said.

'Not all the time.'

She stared at him for a second then sighed. 'I get breathless around you. That's what that is.'

Her confession did something funny to his heart and he tried to make light of it. 'Honesty, Maia?'

'I try to be, when I can.' She too assumed an airiness that didn't fool him in the least. 'Are you honest?'

'I try.' He teased but then sobered. 'You want to know how I feel around you?'

She stilled. Yeah, she did.

'Hungry,' he answered simply. 'Constantly, achingly, ravenously hungry.'

'Gosh, how challenging,' she murmured. 'Maybe it's hormones for you too?'

He laughed softly and pulled her onto his lap. 'Some kind of chemistry for sure.'

It was another hour before they dressed. 'If we're going to walk it needs to be now before that weather hits.'

He kept their pace leisurely, not moving too quickly because he suspected she was more tired than she was willing to admit. He kept his eyes on the sand, scooping up stones occasionally to inspect before either pocketing or tossing them back onto the beach.

'It wasn't to your standards?' she teased. 'You only keep the perfect shells?'

'Not shells, pebbles.' He shot her a smile. 'Olivine. The glassy green ones.'

'You collect them,' she said slowly. 'There's that bowl on the table in the lounge.'

'Yeah.' He shook his head sheepishly. 'Old habit. I used to take the best to my mother.' But some days she'd been too washed out to look at them. 'She would get headaches and we'd come here for a few days. Escape the palace!'

Look after your mother.

'Maybe she just got migraines,' Maia said. 'People do, you know. It might not have had anything to do with the palace. She might have gotten them even if she lived a quiet life in a fishing village on one of the outer islands.'

He shot her a sceptical look. 'Yeah, but I don't think the palace helped.'

'I don't think your *grandparents* helped. Sounds like

they were disapproving taskmasters who put pressure on both your parents.' She shot him a laughing look. 'I don't blame your mother for protecting you from some of that for as long as she could.'

'Protecting me?' He was startled.

'You don't think that's what she was doing?'

'No. She came here to convalesce.'

'Sure, but she brought you too. Maybe she was using her migraines to advantage you both.'

He suddenly smiled. 'You think?'

His grandparents had always disapproved of his time on the island but his mother had insisted that he needed to reconnect with the land and water. She'd been right.

'What happened to your mother?' he asked. It was only fair, right? He'd answered hard questions without wanting to. Without meaning to.

'She walked out when I was very young,' Maia answered. She glanced over at him and sighed. 'She worked on the boat as a steward. They had an affair. I came along—unplanned and not particularly wanted. She would have left him sooner if it weren't for me, I think. But she escaped with another man who abused her worse than my father ever had. He didn't let her contact me for years.' She scooped up a piece of driftwood and ran her fingers over it. 'I guess sometimes it's better the devil you know, right?'

'She didn't try to take you with her?'

'My father wouldn't have let me go. It's not that he actually cared about me, it's just that he's very controlling. He regards people as possessions and he doesn't like to lose any of his possessions. He only likes to accumulate them.'

'And use them.' He sighed.

'I was probably safer being left with Stefan than if I'd gone with her.'

'And she didn't try to help you in all this time?'

'I don't think she can help herself let alone anyone else,' she said quietly. She gazed out across the water. 'I want to do better for this baby.'

'Yeah.' But Niko's bad feeling grew. Her mother had abandoned her. The one true carer in her life had been sent away when she was in her teens and she blamed herself for that. She blamed herself for her mother staying as long as she had with her father too. She felt unwanted. She'd worked hard and long—quietly keeping herself needed, safe. Barely getting the necessities she actually needed. Like basic medical attention. A cold, cold frustration built within him.

'I'm okay, Niko.' She suddenly smiled at him. 'You don't need to try to fix anything. It is what it is.'

'I only want to ensure the baby and you *both* have all you need.'

Maia didn't deserve the difficulties and demands that came with him. His mother hadn't coped with them. His grandmother had built an emotional wall that nothing and no one could get through. But Maia wouldn't have to participate in public life. He could keep her sheltered here. She wouldn't have to work in the way she'd had to all her life.

'We're too far from the house,' he growled as the rain began to fall in large splots. 'We're going to get drenched.'

She chuckled. 'I don't mind.'

He did. He didn't want her slipping. 'Come on. We'll go in there.'

The small shelter was on a slight rise—poles and a roof and only one side, but it was better than nothing.

But inside there was more than he'd realised. There was a small wooden table with three photo frames and a partially burned candle on top. It was neat and so carefully presented. He'd not realised Aron had set those things here—he wouldn't have come in if he had. It was too personal.

'We shouldn't be in here,' Maia said softly.

But Niko was in here now and he couldn't help walking towards that little shrine. His heart ached.

'Who is she?' Maia asked softly, looking at the central picture that he'd been gazing at for long moments. 'A relative?'

'The likeness is obvious, isn't it?' he muttered.

'The cheekbones.' She nodded. 'The nose.'

'Yes.' But he pointed to the other photos first. 'That's Aron's wife. These are my parents.' His father was gazing at his mother as she smiled directly into the camera lens. It said it all to Niko. And he could hardly stand to look at it. So he returned to the photo in the centre. 'That's Lani. Aron's eldest.'

He saw the confusion flickering in Maia's eyes and yeah, it didn't explain the cheekbones. 'She was my grandfather's firstborn. She was born two years before my father. Three years after my grandfather had already married. He was a cheat. He didn't acknowledge her—his illegitimate daughter. He didn't care for her mother. Aron raised her and she became a maid in the palace. Ultimately she worked as my mother's primary attendant, a nanny to me too. We were all very close.'

Maia turned to face him. 'Did you know who she really was? Did *she*?'

'No. Not for all those years. She was denied her name. She was kept in seclusion, a source of shame. Never acknowledged. But never given her freedom either. She missed out on everything she should have had. She didn't get her own damned life. I mean, Aron was wonderful. He tried. So did his wife. But it didn't make up for the fact that she was basically kept as a playmate and then a servant for my father.'

'So that's why you want this child to be legitimate.'

He nodded. 'I would never do that to a child of my own.'

Maia nodded. 'What happened to her?'

'It was coming up to her birthday. She'd always wondered, I think. She'd mention it to Aron sometimes—about how she didn't look like any of her younger siblings. He said nothing, of course. But he couldn't reassure her enough. I think he wanted to tell her but couldn't. She and my mother were very close and they talked about it when we were here. You can see the mirror-image bone structure with my father. I was home for the holidays, full of facts from my marvellous education. Home DNA kits had just hit the market and I suggested that she could get one if she really wanted to find out. She got all excited. She told Aron. And that was when Aron finally told her. I'd forced him into betraying the king.'

'Maybe she should have been told so much sooner,'

Maia said. 'I don't think that's something you ought to feel guilty about.'

Yeah, well. He did. Because it had hurt Aron too. So badly. 'Poor Aron was so loyal. He was doing what was asked of him but I think it tore him up for all those years. He loved Lani, he wanted to protect her. But…' he looked at Maia sadly. 'It shouldn't have happened to her.'

'What happened when Aron told her?'

'Dad was away—he didn't know Aron had said anything. My grandfather was at our house in the hills. Lani wanted to confront him—right away. And my mother offered to go with her.' Of course she'd offered. She'd cared deeply. 'Mum said she'd drive. I asked if she had a headache and she said she didn't, but I could tell. So I should have stopped her. I knew those headaches affected her vision and it was always my job to look after her when she had one.' His father had always told him to. 'I should have stopped them both. They should have waited until the morning. They were both so upset and they left.' He shook his head. 'Mum drove the coastal road. She missed a corner.'

'Oh, Niko.'

Yeah. 'They both died.'

'How did your father cope?'

'He didn't. He stopped caring about anything. Especially himself. I never saw him sober again and he hardly saw me at all. He sent me back to boarding school. He blamed me for her death and he never recovered from it.' He stared at the image of man who'd loved too much to live without his wife. 'He banished Aron. My grandfather was furious but he just clammed up even more. He wouldn't talk about it. Ever. And he expected Dad to be stoic and get on with the job. But Dad just never recovered from losing the love of his life. He was stuck in hellish grief. He made a bunch of poor choices, ended up with high blood pressure, high sugars and only a couple years later had a fatal stroke when he was far too young. My grandfather lost both his children right before each turned forty.'

'I'm so sorry, Niko.'

'Yeah.' He sighed. 'It sucked.'

She stood for a moment, then moved to the table and took a match from the box, lighting the candle that Aron had there.

'You know it wasn't your fault, right? Not any of it.' She turned once the flame had steadied. 'It wasn't fair of him to blame you like that.'

He swallowed hard and tried to smile. 'Life isn't fair though, is it? You know that too.'

She looked up so softly. 'I'm still sorry all that happened.'

He nodded. They stood for a long time, just watching the candle flicker.

'The rain's stopped.' He'd realised eventually. 'We should go back while it holds.'

He blew out the flame and they walked back in silence. Back at the house he felt oddly unsure of what to do with himself. But Maia went into the lounge and came back out to the pool area with something in her hand.

'Want to play poker?' She looked at him with limpid eyes.

He stared, nonplussed. But in the next second vitality warmed his veins and a helpless laugh escaped him. 'Maia...'

She smiled at him. So beautiful, so sweet and she nodded towards the pile on the table where he'd emptied his pockets. 'I'll play for your stones.'

'True treasure. Very wise.' His mood lightened. 'But what are *you* going to put on the table?'

She shot him an arch look. 'My knife.'

'Wow, bold.' He took a seat with a smile. 'You're feeling confident, then.'

She shrugged, then winked. Easiness blossomed and her distraction—he knew it was that—worked. She brought him back to here and now and it was okay. Maybe this whole thing between them could be okay.

She was a card shark of course. There was no way she'd spent so long on a gambling boat and not learned some tricks. But her pleasure in beating him was a pleasure for him in itself. He watched as she carefully pawed through the little stones, picking out several of a similar size. 'These are going to be perfect,' she muttered.

He shook his head. He hadn't realised she really wanted them. 'You know I would have just given them to you if you'd asked.'

She glanced up at him, surprise sparkling in her beautiful eyes. 'You would?'

He blinked. 'Of course.'

Maia sat with her feet curled beneath her, pointlessly whittling a new-found piece of wood that was rapidly becoming shavings and nothing else. She'd come close to cutting herself accidentally twice in the last two minutes. Something she hadn't done in years. But the man beside her was an appalling distraction. He was sprawled back on the cushions beside the pool, ignoring the papers scattered beside him to feast his eyes on her like a sexually satisfied sultan from centuries ago. But he was more than that. He was a nice guy who'd been so hurt. He'd suffered loss after loss after loss and had guilt piled on him when he didn't deserve it. And here he was trying so hard to do what was right. He didn't want to repeat any mistakes of the past. He wanted his child acknowledged. He wanted to ensure both she and the baby were well cared for because he felt as if he'd failed to do that for others in the past. And that was all so very honourable. But somehow she felt more uncertain about everything.

It was five days since he'd brought her here. Four nights in which she'd slept not just in a bed, but in his arms. Three days of absolute pleasure. But more than that—there'd been laughter. There'd been companionship of a kind she'd never really had. And she didn't quite know how to handle it.

'I'll get you some better wood if you want?' he offered.

'No, that's not the point.' She smiled. 'The joy is in making something out of nothing very much, you know? And it doesn't matter if you muck it up because you can just throw it away because it was just scrap anyway.'

'Is that what you do with them?' He sounded outraged. 'You just throw them away?'

'Well, no,' she admitted sheepishly. 'I leave them in little places. Then look for them if ever I go back.'

'Like a calling card?'

'More like secret graffiti—*Maia was here*—but only I know.' And only she cared really.

'In, like, ports?'

'On beaches mostly.' She bent closer to focus on creating a decent beak for the little bird. But once again she missed. 'Damn.'

His chuckle made her glance up. He had the oddest expression in his eyes.

'What?' she asked, then almost cut herself again.

'No one's going to be surprised to learn you're pregnant.'

'What? Why?' She put her hand to her belly but it seemed as not-quite-flat as it had been the day before.

'Anyone who sees you is going to know how thoroughly you've been...'

She glanced back up at him sharply. 'Been?'

The word was crude but appallingly it turned her on anyway.

'You look like you've spent hours in bed yet not slept a wink,' he elaborated lazily. Leaning close he brushed her hair back over her shoulder. 'Your hair is wild, you have a kiss-swollen mouth, two love bites on your neck and yet your nipples are still screaming at me through that bikini top. You look ravished and ready for more.'

He sat back looking too smug. The flare of lust that had shot through her suddenly iced. Was *that* why he'd slept with her—why he'd been so passionate? So people would take one look at her and know she'd been his sexual plaything?

His gaze narrowed. 'For the record, the look suits you. Very much. You have colour in your cheeks and sparkle in your eyes and you look ten times more alive than you did the morning I took you from that tinpot boat.'

'Gosh. I'm flattered,' she said coldly. 'Isn't that a marvellously convenient side effect of your sexual skills? To make it look convincing to the world that yes, you've seduced this woman and oh look, now she's pregnant,' she groused. 'But I'm so sorry you felt you *had* to do that.'

'Maia.' He gaped at her.

Yes, she was grumpy. She was unaccountably, incredibly grumpy and yes, she was kicking off. But she needed to push this because she'd suddenly realised this isolated lust-fest wasn't necessarily *real*. At least, not for him.

'Did you sleep with me so you can sell your paternity story? Was it all about proving your virility?'

'Are you serious right now?'

Yes, she was. It suddenly all made sense. He'd only bought her to the island to create a narrative about their 'love' story. To have the world believe in them as a couple. It was calculating and she felt so naive. He was probably desperate to get back to his city life and not have to spend all these hours entertaining her. He'd probably been *bored*.

But *she* hadn't been. She'd laughed—she'd loved those long hours in bed when he'd taken so much time with her. But she'd read all of that wrong. He was only doing what he had to do, to get what he wanted. And when would she ever learn that people didn't stick around for her for long?

'You don't want anyone to know the truth about the conception,' she said.

'Well, I don't particularly want our child growing up believing they were a sheer fluke thanks to fate.'

'No one should ever know,' she said.

'Hopefully they won't.'

'But if they did, it shouldn't matter.'

'But it *would*. This child's paternity would be open to question. But that's not really an issue now, is it? Given we *are* lovers, Maia.'

'You seduced me only so you can say that.' This was all a cover for the baby.

'Don't be ridiculous.' He glared at her. 'And maybe we ought to clarify who seduced who, Maia.'

'As if I had any control over you?' she said. 'But now you've gotten that mundane task out of the way, perhaps we can move on.'

'Maia—'

'What? There's no need for us to remain here now you've had me every way you want.'

'I haven't actually,' he purred. 'There are lots of positions we've yet to explore with each other and there is no way I've *taught* you everything you need to know in bed.'

She was not being derailed by that thought. She was calling a halt to it now. 'Tough. We're done.'

'*What?*'

'I want to go back to the city,' she said firmly.

He stared, wariness flickering in his eyes before he stiffened. She knew then that he didn't want her to go there. Not back to the palace. Why did he want to keep her isolated? Was he afraid she would embarrass him somehow? Her horror simply deepened.

'You can stay here. You're safe and free to do anything you like here.'

'Swim, sleep and have sex? I want more than that.' She was furious that he was trying to block her. She would fight for the lifestyle she'd longed for. 'I've been shut away below deck for most of my life. The last thing I want is to be shut away on a remote, unpopulated island for the next who knows how long. Even if it is a paradise island, it's still a kind of prison. I won't let you hide me away like some shameful secret. I want to do things. See things. I want to *breathe*.'

She wanted independence and liberty. She wanted to go shopping. She'd never been paid. Never had money. She wanted a job. There were so many things she'd never had and never done.

His expression had turned stormy. 'You're saying this isn't enough.'

'No. It's not.' Her nerves tightened but she needed this. It felt good to declare her needs. To put her own desires as her priority—for the first time in her life. Even so, she braced for his explosion.

He regarded her intently. 'Fine. That's fair enough.'

She glanced up, startled that he'd agreed so swiftly.

'We'll return to the city. See if you like palace life better this time round. You're the one who ran away, remember?' He tugged on a T-shirt with jerky movements. 'It's hardly been a walk in the park for me either by the way. Trying to run my country from a remote island. Disappearing and not turning up to events that have been scheduled months in advance.'

'I'm so sorry *your* life has been so inconvenienced,' she said sarcastically. 'But as it happens you're not the only one. I have the ultimate accidental pregnancy going on.'

CHAPTER ELEVEN

NIKO DIDN'T KNOW what to think. Somehow an off-hand remark had caused a combustion of epic proportions. But if Maia wanted more, she would get more. It took nothing to make the arrangements. In less than an hour they'd helicoptered back to the palace—returning to formality, to constraint, to all those rules, too quickly. But he would show exactly how willing he was and far he would go to look after her and keep her happy.

'There's a gala tonight,' he coolly informed her the minute they were left alone in the suite he'd insisted she be accommodated in. The one right alongside his. 'I'd intended to send my apologies but you can come with me instead. I'll never be ashamed to be seen with you, Maia.'

She looked unsure. 'A gala?'

'A variety performance. Singing. Music. I think some dance, I can't remember all the exact details.'

'Like the theatre?'

'Yes, the theatre,' he snapped.

Her eyes suddenly brightened. 'I've never been to the theatre.'

Speechless, he stared, his anger instantly swamped

by the desire to see her reaction to such an entertainment. And by bitterness that she'd not been before. Something else brewed deeper. He'd wanted to keep her safe and honestly he still didn't know if there was a direct threat either to him or to her given what had happened at the medical centre. He'd wanted time for Pax to complete his investigation. Only now she'd had enough of the island and he refused to keep her prisoner there.

'I might need to go shopping,' she said apologetically. 'For underwear at least. Will one of the beach dresses do?'

'No,' he muttered. 'I'll come with you.'

'You don't have to,' she said annoyingly quickly. 'I'm not going to try to run away.'

He gritted his teeth but failed to stop the resurgence of his temper. 'I know that.'

'Did you want to vet my choices?' she suddenly flared. 'What if I promise only to get clothing that will show off how thoroughly I've been...*seduced*.'

'That sounds perfect,' he snapped. 'We'll start with evening dresses. Backless and braless.'

'Of course, Your Highness.' She dropped a mocking curtsey. 'Your wish is my command.'

His jaw tightened. She seemed determined to take *everything* the wrong way and he was beyond frustrated that everything seemed to becoming more complicated by the hour. He missed the easy alignment they'd had only yesterday. He'd wanted to see she was safe. And he'd wanted to see her have some *fun*. Instead he'd been provoked into retaliating and she was huffier than ever. He needed to kiss her. Now.

'Your Highness?'

He whirled away from her as an assistant called through the door. An interruption. Of course. That was life in the palace. Constant interruptions. Constant demands when all he wanted was to be alone with her.

So he *would* go with her to those shops. He would snatch any moment he could have with her.

An hour later Maia tried to keep her chin in the air as she walked out of the dressing room but she was inwardly baulking at how revealing the dress she'd furiously swished off the rack actually was. Ordinarily she never would have picked one like this. Both low and high cut and skin-tight, she wouldn't have the confidence to wear it in *public* in a million years. In a bedroom however? Well, *that* was a possibility. Doing this to aggravate Niko was likely to backfire yet she couldn't seem to stop herself.

Niko took one look at her, whirled on his heel and barked at the hovering assistants. 'Empty the store. Leave. Now. All of you.'

She gaped. 'You can't just—'

He spun back and pulled her against him before she even had the idea to step back. 'I am the king. I can do whatever the hell I want,' he growled.

'Really?'

'Yes.' His lips traversed the edge of the dress, the high crest of her breast. 'And I want to do you.'

It would take only a nudge of the fabric and her nipple would be exposed. But Niko didn't nudge—he slid his hand beneath the skirt and up to where she ached instead.

'Spoilt, Niko,' she hissed, scandalised even as she

spread her legs for him. It was appalling to consider how little she truly cared when all she wanted was him to touch her like this—to want her as desperately as she still wanted him. She needed this contact. Her head fell back as he kissed her neck, but as her eyes drifted shut she spotted something and froze. 'There are security cameras.'

'Williams will have the footage deleted,' Niko slurred recklessly and then a gleam entered his eye. 'Or give it to me.'

He kissed her—his tongue circling, his *finger* circling. It was too much, too soon and she was so close to coming apart. She gasped and clasped his shoulders, shivering as she tore her mouth free while pressing her hips nearer to him. '*Niko...*'

She needed to be alone with him. She ached for the release, she wanted the luxury of time and space—for once she longed for an actual bed. *Now.*

He dragged in a sharp breath, stilling momentarily. Then he suddenly dropped his hand. 'You're right,' he said huskily. 'I apologise. I'll leave you to finish choosing your dress for tonight. *Alone.*'

He remained only long enough to ensure she had her balance. She barely did. Because she'd never felt as angry. But he left the shop without a backwards glance.

Captain Williams appeared to accompany her mere seconds later. Scary, silent, stupidly wearing those sunglasses inside. Only once had she caught a glimpse of his eyes—so ice blue they were almost colourless. He had a scar too, so maybe that was why he wore the sunglasses. She felt bad for her mean thought. She couldn't ask him. He wasn't exactly someone she could confide in.

'The king is not used to not getting what he wants,' the taciturn soldier said. 'It's good for him.' He took up position near the door. '*You're* good for him.'

Maia was too surprised to answer. The man never spoke and he certainly shouldn't be commenting on that. Plus he couldn't be more wrong.

It wasn't her job to be 'good' for King Niko. Honestly, they just seemed to bring worse out in each other the more time they spent together.

Niko struggled to stay still while the barber clipped his hair. 'Oh, just leave it,' he snapped irritably, waving the man away from him.

He'd not recovered since returning to the palace over two hours ago. How had he lost all control as to start pawing her in the middle of a *shop*? Why hadn't she returned yet? Why had they left the island? Why had he agreed so swiftly instead of staying calm and convincing her to stay? They could have indulged this bone-deep lust until it was exhausted at last. Whenever the hell that was going to be.

The moment Pax walked in without knocking Niko growled. 'What took so long?'

'Ms Flynn was enjoying herself,' the soldier answered expressionlessly. 'Wasn't that what you wanted?'

Honestly, Niko just wanted her back beside him and he was too annoyed with everything to shoot Pax a quelling look. 'Where is she now?'

'Finishing dressing. She asked me to tell you she won't take long.'

Niko breathed a little more easily. He glanced at the barber hurriedly packing away his tools and regretted his short fuse.

'I apologise.' He never took his temper out on his staff. He never felt this irritable. Ever. 'Forgive me, please. I'm just...' He paused and reached for the right word. '*Nervous.*'

The barber looked startled, then offered a wary smile. 'Of course, Your Highness.'

Niko knew full well the palace gossip machine would be in full swing in two minutes on the basis of that comment. Frankly, it wasn't a lie. He was feeling edgy. And regretful. But now they were running late and they didn't have the time to talk through strategy for the evening. Maybe this way was best. If she were overwhelmed with information she might want to bail. She didn't understand the consequences of being seen out with him in this context. And his admission of nerves just then? That he was taking her to the theatre? It was as good as a declaration nailed to the palace wall.

Ten minutes later he knocked on her door. 'I'm sorry, Maia,' he ground out. 'There's not much time before we're...'

He lost everything except vision as she opened the door. Thank the gods he kept that because the gorgeous coral dress hugged her breasts then fell in a stunning swathe to the floor, skimming the slight curve of her belly without betraying her secret. It was so much more 'palace appropriate' than the revealing number from the shop but it seduced him as swiftly. Reduced him. He was nothing more than a man unbearably aching for the woman in front of him.

He just wanted to rip it off her.

He could make them delay the performance. He could be as late as he liked. But she'd called him self-ish once already today and he didn't fancy a repeat of that loss of control. Because she was right and he was ashamed because he'd not been thinking about anything other than how much he wanted to touch her.

'It will only take me a moment to finish,' she said.

Yeah? It would take him less time to finish exactly the way he wanted to.

But he didn't. He could—*would*—resist. This wasn't a test only for her, he realised. It was for him as well.

As he'd suspected the message to the barber had had its intended effect. The entire palace staff were lined up for his departure.

'No wonder you're big-headed,' Maia murmured as they briefly paused at the top of the stair to take in the liveried display. 'Does this happen every time you leave your own house?'

A chuckle escaped him.

'What's so funny?'

He couldn't tell her yet.

The audience stood as they entered the theatre—last of course. And they stared. He held her hand as they were guided to their seats. It was another word-less declaration and yes, caused a massive murmur to ripple throughout the auditorium. Then a burst of thun-derous applause. She glanced at him and he just knew she was wishing she could roll her eyes at his perceived pomposity. He just smiled at her, feeling guilty that she didn't even know their fate was sealed.

'Thank you for singing the anthem so beautifully,' he turned his head to mutter when they finally took their seats.

'Well, I wasn't about to flub it with the whole world watching.' She spoke without moving her lips an impressive skill he personally found very useful. 'Though to be honest I'm amazed I actually knew all the words.'

He laughed, releasing a speck of the tension that had been riding him hard. But then the performance began and another tension consumed him. He tried so hard, but he couldn't stop himself watching her. She wasn't just absorbed in the performances, she was *entranced*. And he?

He was no better than an animal fixated on his next feed. He'd drag her away at half-time if he could— but he couldn't do it to her. She was luminous—loving every moment—while he endured the pleasure and pain of watching her but not touching her.

The minute they were alone he was apologising to her. Then he was kissing her.

He would take all that he could, when he could.

Maia had never felt so self-conscious. There'd been an insane number of people lined up in the palace to see King Niko off, but it was nothing compared to the entire audience staring up at him now. Most had repeatedly glanced up at him throughout the performance instead of watching the action onstage. One woman dressed in blue just a few rows away hadn't taken her eyes off him for the entire time. Of course, Maia didn't blame her. He looked devastating in that crisp white shirt and black trousers. He'd shaved, showing off the cheekbones that gave her palpitations. More handsome, more rakish than ever.

'You enjoyed it?' he asked as he guided her into the small room behind the royal box in the theatre.

'I've never seen anything like it.' And she was relieved to have a moment without everyone watching.

'We're expected to go backstage to meet some of the cast.' He watched her with amusement. 'Would you like that?'

'Of course, if that's what's expected.'

'But would you like it?'

'Yes.' She smiled at him. 'Those singers were amazing. I'd like to tell them how much I enjoyed their performance.'

He nodded and she moved to exit the small room.

'Stop,' he breathed harshly and grabbed her arm. 'Stay a moment.'

She looked up at him, startled.

'I want to apologise,' he muttered. 'I was a jerk to you today. I just wanted to see you having fun. I wanted to be in on it. But of course you should have been free to go just…find what you wanted on your own. I'm sorry I wrecked that for you.'

Her heart thudded. *That* was why he'd wanted to go with her? Why hadn't he said so at the time?

'I wish we hadn't left the island so soon.' He groaned.

In this second so did she. Sexual attraction was a storm—it was like being picked up by gale force winds and carried away with no control, no ability to decide her direction…but she was so glad he seemed to want her equally intensely. 'I'm sorry too.'

'No—'

'Your Highness?' a voice called from beyond the curtain.

Niko released her and smiled. 'Let's go meet the stars.'

He introduced her as his friend. She smiled—knowing enough from the stewards on her father's boat to carry her through. She voiced her appreciation politely but genuinely to each performer. The woman in the blue dress was there with the dignitaries. Still staring.

But Niko had them out of there in record time.

Back at the palace it was as if they'd entered some sci-fi film in which every other human had vanished off the face of the earth.

'I'm astonished there isn't a welcome party waiting for you.' She gazed around the vast emptiness in amazement.

He chuckled. 'I requested that they give us privacy upon our return.'

'Everyone really stares at you all of the time, don't they?'

'Perk of the job.'

She shot him a laughing glance. 'I'm not feeling sorry for you.'

'I never imagined for a second that you were.' He angled his head. 'You enjoyed it tonight?'

'Very much, actually. The concert, that is. Not so much the staring. Did you notice the woman in the blue dress? She didn't stop staring your way the entire night.'

'Blue dress?' He frowned, then suddenly froze as recognition jolted into his eyes. 'Oh.'

'Oh?' She paused, reading awkwardness in his expression.

But then he swallowed and lifted his head. 'She's the partner of the bass player of that international band. We knew each other a few years ago when I was visiting New Zealand.'

She understood immediately. 'You were intimate?'

'Briefly.'

The blue-dress beauty was a former lover and while she might be someone else's partner now, she clearly still had eyes for Niko. Again, Maia didn't blame her.

But the blue-dress beauty was a woman Niko had *chosen*. Maia wasn't. She was literally a vessel. The fertile recipient of a shocking error. Fate had twisted them together in some Machiavellian amusement for reasons unknown. And Maia was wholly unsuitable to be his bride. 'You should have told me earlier.'

'So you could avoid her?'

Maia flicked her hair. 'So I could swap notes.'

A half smile creased his mouth. 'Jealous?'

'No,' she lied.

'To be honest I'd forgotten she might be there. To be completely honest I'd forgotten *her*.'

'Is that supposed to make me think more of you?'

'You're the only woman I'll marry.'

She still wasn't sure about that at all. 'If I do marry you, it will only be because of a mistake.'

'And yet I can't keep my hands off you.' He advanced on her.

'You have a high sex drive. It's nothing to do with me.'

His smile finally faded. 'And what about you? Have you just discovered your own high sex drive? Does that have nothing to do with *me*?' He shook his head. 'This is *us*, Maia. This is only like this between *us*. You and me.'

Her pulse thundered. 'You said we were just burning this out.'

'Yeah, well. Maybe I was wrong.'

'You're the king,' she goaded. Driven—yet again—by that inner demon who lived to provoke him. 'You're never wrong.'

'I'm *human*, Maia. And as you know more than anyone, I don't always perform at my best. Especially around—' He sighed heavily. 'I'm volatile around you.'

'You don't like that.'

'It's unusual,' he clipped.

'I guess this is an unusual set of circumstances.'

'Do you know, I don't actually think it is the circumstances,' he said. 'I think it's just you.'

'Then perhaps I should go.'

His hands landed heavily on her waist. 'You're not bloody going anywhere.'

She tossed her head as the fire ignited. *This* was what she'd wanted. To push him into pulling her closer.

'Nobody has ever driven me crazy the way you do.' He stared at her for a long moment.

She squirmed as he read the hunger she knew she couldn't hide. And sure enough he suddenly smiled.

'You don't have to taunt me into sleeping with you, Maia,' he lazily leaned closer to whisper hot and rough in her ear. 'I will do this with you anytime. Just bat your lashes. Crook your damned little finger. Lick your lips. Anything. I will pleasure you anytime you want. Because I want you incessantly. Endlessly. All the *bloody* time.'

Primal satisfaction surged at his admission of uncontrolled desire and in seconds she melted. They sank where they were, barely beyond the doorway of his suite. He stripped away the soft coral silk and dragged in a stunned breath when he saw the lace underwear she'd enjoyed choosing with him in mind. His reaction was everything she'd wanted. Because in seconds the underwear was gone and he was between her legs, stroking her to searing heights. She liked the danger of him. The strength. The way he moved to hold her as if he would never let her go. As if she could never, ever escape. 'But I like taunting you…'

'Well then, my sweet little vixen, you'd better be prepared for the consequences.'

He flipped her over and lifted her to her knees. She gasped, stunned as he moved behind her. Desire ignited as he touched her in ways she'd never imagined. She was so hot and he was so wicked.

'What are you doing?' she moaned helplessly, so, so close. 'Why have you stopped?'

His smile was pure devilishness.

She batted her lashes. She crooked her little finger. She licked her lips.

And with each invitation he rewarded her—with attention, with kisses, strokes, teases, but never giving her enough to let her have her release.

'Niko!' she gasped in lustful outrage and desperation.

'Ask me nicely,' he dared. 'Just this once.'

Breathless she twisted from his hold and lay back

on the floor, inviting him with her spread legs, with the arch of her hips, with the sweep of her hands across her breasts and down her body…in an effort to tempt him into loss of control. In an effort to get what she needed all on her own.

But he swiped her hands away with a devilish laugh. 'Oh no, my darling. That pleasure is for another day. Today you only come on *my* touch.'

She met his playful gaze and conceded everything. 'Then touch me. *Please.*'

He didn't just touch her. He took her—hard. Her orgasm was instant. She cried out—shocked at the intensity. But he kissed her through the comedown, then laced his fingers through hers and slowly built her up again. The connection was intimate and enduring. He rocked into her over and over, somehow pressing closer and closer still. His gaze bored into hers—with soft amusement, such tenderness and savage tension.

'It wasn't so hard, was it?' he choked. 'You're all I can think about.'

He was locked so deeply inside her that she felt the rigidity in every inch of him.

'My beautiful Maia.'

This time she finally believed him. This time she revelled in a release unlike anything ever.

She was so spent he had to carry her to his bed. So spent she couldn't even open her eyes. She'd thought he wouldn't hurt her. And he absolutely wouldn't. Not deliberately. But suddenly she understood how deeply he *could*. He made her believe she was beautiful. He'd made her feel wanted. And now, in the aftermath of such total ecstasy, her heart ached for even more. And suddenly she was restless again, like she'd been that first night, but this time for different—far scarier—reasons.

In the darkness Niko chuckled softly. 'Come here.'

He pulled her tightly into his arms, knowing her too well. And as he stroked her hair, he took her heart deeper into his clutches with every caress.

CHAPTER TWELVE

'MAIA.'

She stirred then came awake swiftly. 'What's wrong?' Maia wrapped the sheet around herself as she sat up.

Niko's jaw was looking particularly angular this morning.

'It seems your father is unhappy,' he said. 'He's been making this known across town. Spreading the news that his daughter has been abducted by the king to be his sex slave.'

She gaped, her cheeks burning. 'You're not serious.'

'I'm going to speak to him,' he said shortly. 'Williams has brought him downstairs.'

'Don't see him,' Maia said quickly. 'I don't care what he says. I don't care what anyone thinks.' She looked at Niko's deepening frown. 'But you do.'

'I am the king, Maia. I must uphold certain standards.'

'But no one is ever going to believe him.' She tried to laugh it off. 'Like *you* need to abduct anyone?'

'I did exactly that though, didn't I?' He stared at her moodily. 'It's one thing to be seen as a playboy. It's quite another to be seen as a sex offender.'

'But you're not.' Her lungs constricted but still she tried to offer another smile. 'I...was willing.'

'Were you?' He didn't smile back at her. 'What choices did I give you really?'

'Every choice that matters.' She lifted her head proudly. 'I slept with you because I wanted to. I could have said no but I didn't want to. In fact I think you're right and I might have started it. And I have no regrets.' She looked at him, her heart quaking. 'Do you?'

He didn't answer. 'I *must* announce our engagement, Maia. It's past time.'

'No.' Maia rejected the idea immediately. After last night there was no way she could marry him. 'No, Niko.'

'To be frank it's already done, Maia. Our going out together last night was as good as any formal engagement announcement. That's why the staff all lined up to see you leave with me. They know their king has selected his bride.'

'*No.*' Her jaw dropped. 'That's not possible.'

'There's a reason you've never seen me on a date here in Piri-nu, Maia.' His lips twisted ruefully. 'The smallest signals are taken very seriously.'

'Being seen in public with a woman doesn't make it imperative that you marry her. That's ridiculous.' She didn't want to marry him. Not like this. Not because of this. 'I don't want to marry you, Niko. It's not necessary.' She swung out of bed and hurriedly tugged on some underwear. 'I'll see my father and tell him to stop. You needn't concern yourself. It's not your job.'

'When it's my name he's slandering?'

'It's mine too and he's *my* father.' Once more her father's interference was impacting on her life. Because of him she was not good enough to be Niko's bride. She would see him now and tell him to leave.

'I'm not letting you face him alone.' Niko folded his arms and watched her tug down the sundress she'd grabbed.

'I don't need protection.' She stilled with the strangest, most sudden certainty.

She felt oddly free from fear of her father. She could—would—hold her ground and she would not let him destroy what she had with Niko. Even if it were only for now. There was nothing he could do to her *personally* now.

'Maybe I want to be there only to make sure your father doesn't instantly die from the daggers in your eyes.' Niko finally smiled. 'It won't be easy but I promise I won't interrupt. But I would like just to be there.' He drew a deep breath. 'But it can be Williams if you prefer.'

She didn't particularly want Niko there but she infinitely preferred him to Captain Scary-silent. 'You can stand at the back. *Quietly.*' She turned. 'I'll see him off now.'

She would get it over with before this rush of confidence left her. But oddly it didn't. She was calmer than she would ever have imagined she could be when facing her father and openly defying him for the first time in her life.

The ruddy-faced man glared at her as she walked in but it wasn't her he addressed.

'You have to marry her. You've ruined her.'

Maia saw the glint of avariciousness in her father's

eyes and knew she was nothing but a pawn to him—a possession. A thing to be bartered and to make money from. Because it was always all about money with him. Money and control.

'What century do you think we're living in?' she asked coolly. 'I wanted to leave the boat and King Niko graciously enabled me to do that. He's shown me nothing but kindness and generosity and you're to stop the rubbish interpretation you're spreading around town. It's not true.'

Her father laughed. 'As if you're not warming his bed every night?'

She held her head high with sheer grit. 'I'm a free woman and I've no intention of marrying anyone at this stage of my life.'

'So you're happy to be his whore?'

She saw Niko's involuntary step forward out of the corner of her eye and lifted her hand in a quelling gesture without taking her attention from her father. 'Don't try to slut-shame me. I've done nothing wrong. Certainly nothing *illegal*.' She paused for effect before asking him coolly, 'Can you say the same?'

His eyes narrowed and he walked closer to speak directly to her. 'Are you not going to try to take advantage of this situation, you stupid girl?' he hissed sharply. 'Don't you understand what we could achieve here? I'm trying to *help* you. At the very least you could get money—'

'May I advise you to stay out of Piri-nu waters, Father,' she said firmly, overriding his attempt to convince her. 'I think the stakes in some of your games might exceed the laws here. I'd hate for you to be caught out by that.'

'You wouldn't—'

'And I won't. If you leave right away.' She made herself smile. Made herself believe that this didn't matter.

'You're even more useless than your mother.'

'Goodbye, Dad, I don't expect we'll see each other much in the future.' Maia turned her back on him to walk from the room while she still could.

'Maia!' He yelled her name the same way he'd yelled it her whole life. 'You can't walk away—'

She paused. 'Actually, I can.'

'You'll regret not taking my help,' he sneered. 'He'll tire of you. You have nothing. You are nothing and you'll end up with nothing.'

At that she turned to look at him one last time. 'And you offered me so very much more?' She shrugged. 'I have more than you right now. I have the one thing I'll never let myself lose. My *integrity.*'

The one thing her father had never had in the first place.

She would be true to herself. She walked out of the room, no longer caring who heard, whether Niko was with her or not. She marched straight back to the suite she'd shared with him last night.

Five minutes later the door opened and Niko entered the room.

'Are you okay?' He walked slowly towards her as if wary of her mood.

'Did you threaten him?' she asked.

'No more than you already had,' he replied. 'He

wasn't interested in sticking around to talk to me. I think he was surprised by you.'

Because she'd always been so compliant. Because she'd never stood up for herself before. For so long she'd simply accepted her fate.

But it was because of Niko that she now could. Because of this impossible mess that she finally had one element of freedom. Now she would push for everything. *Nothing* mattered more.

She looked at him. 'I'm not going to marry you, Niko.'

His expression hardened. 'I don't think—'

'You can consider me your concubine, but I will never be your bride,' she added.

'My *what*?' He halted, startled.

'Concubine. It's an apt word. Evokes a sort of decadence that's perfect for you.' And *them*—the passion they shared for now at least.

'Maia—'

'You can declare our child your heir without us being married. You're the king. You know you can do this.'

'I don't want to.'

'But you can. There would be no question.'

'Is the thought of marrying me really so distasteful?'

She actually couldn't *bear* the thought of being married to him. She would be his lover—happily, for as long as they were both interested in that element of their relationship. She would always be the mother of his firstborn child. But she should *never* be his wife. She couldn't cope with that.

Because she was so far in love with him it was cruel. She wasn't good enough. The last twenty minutes had cemented that fact. For a moment there she'd thought she was. Her father had ruined it. But the reminder was a good thing. Everyone would have found out soon enough anyway.

'Thanks to my father the world now knows I share your bed.' She tossed her head. 'They know I'm your lover. Soon enough they'll know I'm going to be the mother of your heir. That is *enough*.'

'You must let me give you the protection of my name. They'll vilify you.'

'I know you care what they will say about me. But you also know they'll only say even more if I were to become your *wife*.' She shook her head. 'It's too permanent, Niko. As your lover I'll be tolerated. Not as your wife. I'm not the right choice. I'm not your equal. Not in any way. And as for my father…my mother…' She shook her head at him. 'You never would have chosen to be with me if it weren't for everything and we both know it.'

He stared at her, an obstinate expression building in his eyes. 'How we met is irrelevant. We must do what is right.'

'But marriage *isn't* right,' she argued all over again. 'If we do it this way, then there won't be any kind of perceived *failure*. No public end of a relationship or the breaking of promises made. There's just been a liaison and an accident. I am your lover. I know there will be no escape for good, Niko. I'll always be near the palace. We'll always be part of each other's lives. We have to be because of this baby. But you and I, this intimacy, will end eventually, you know it will.'

He suddenly paused, whirling to face her. 'Is that

why *you* did it?' he questioned sharply. 'Did you give me your virginity so you could cast yourself as a seductress?'

Maia stilled, suddenly hurt. Suddenly scared. He had no idea, did he. Of how she really felt. And perhaps that was for the best. 'I—'

Niko turned at the bloody knock on the door. 'What is it?' he snapped.

But he took one look at Williams' face and walked out of the room to speak with him in the corridor. Frankly he needed the breathing space from Maia's defiance. Her *luminescence*. The quiet dignity in her declaration of her integrity had stunned him. More stunning was her display of power and serenity since. Her sudden stubbornness that he had the sinking feeling he wasn't going to be able to sway. She was rejecting him. And he was suddenly incensed because *she* wouldn't see sense.

'What is it, Pax?' he asked heavily.

'The investigation into the medical facility is complete.'

Niko stiffened. 'And?'

'Genuine mistake,' Pax confirmed. 'It was the same clinician who retrieved the wrong sample and who treated Maia in the rooms. She isn't well herself. Her vision. But she was hiding her declining eyesight because she needed the job.'

'Money?' Niko slumped against the wall and bowed his head.

'Family commitments, yes.'

'Poor woman.' Niko didn't have it in him to be angry with someone other than Maia right now and certainly didn't have the heart for recriminations. 'Is she okay?'

'She's distraught. I've asked that she gets professional support. They're revising their storage processes of course and upgrading the technology. It was an appalling chain of events unlikely ever to be repeated.'

'So it wasn't some kind of threat, no sick sort of succession plot to create an heir?' Niko double-checked.

Pax shook his head. 'I shook the tree hard, but there's nothing.'

'Which means there's no threat to Maia from this?'

'Not from this, now.'

'Any other threats to her?'

'Nothing aside from the interest generated from her appearance with you last night. That's only going to heighten over the coming months.'

Niko gritted his teeth. 'Thanks, you can go.'

Pax said nothing more and walked down the corridor. But Niko didn't go back into the room where Maia was waiting. He paused just outside the door, trying to wrap his head around the confusion of the last twenty-four hours. None of this was as simple as he'd thought it could be.

Last night he'd felt contrarian. Wanting to show her off and hide her away at the same time. It was the zillionth time he'd seen such a performance but the first for her, and seeing her so sweetly transfixed by the show had brought him immense pleasure. Frankly he'd forgotten Athena was going to be there last night. He'd forgotten most of the women he'd been with. He hadn't thought about another woman in days. He'd had his hands too full coping with Maia.

The contradictory feelings were so freaking complicated and he couldn't straighten them out. And the anxiety underlying it all was rising. Niko didn't do anxiety. He did certainty. He was good at it. So this was very weird and very uncomfortable.

But the fact was any danger Maia now might face was purely because of him. She was losing her freedom because of him. Her life would be irrevocably changed because of him.

None of this was what she would have chosen for herself. Ever. And she didn't want it. She was pushing to put herself in the position of his lover. To reduce herself—shrink inwards and accept less than she ought to ever have. Because that was what she was used to.

Meeting her father had sickened him. Worse was the realisation that he wanted the same outcome as that man. To be aligned in any way with that the guy seemed wrong. But they wanted the same thing for vastly different reasons, right?

Her father was a man in power telling her what to do. Telling her he knew best. That he wanted only to 'help' her. Not listening to her at all. Hearing that cruel tone, the coercion, the manipulation had made him realise that he was doing the exact same thing.

He really wasn't as different to Brant Flynn as he'd liked to think. They were both men taking advantage of what authority they had to get what they wanted. All but haggling over her. Not letting her choose.

The levels of control she'd been subjected to her whole life were exhausting. Everyone had things they *had* to do, that was part of life but Maia hadn't had the most basic of freedoms nor the chance to discover things for herself. She'd never had normal *options*. So how could she know what she really wanted when she'd never had the time or space to figure it out for herself?

But one thing she'd made clear was that she didn't want to marry him. He'd been trying to convince her from the start and she wouldn't budge—today she was more vehement, more calm about it, than ever.

And now he felt unsure that the intimacy they'd shared had only happened because she'd felt some innate need to protect herself. That she'd wanted to please him and thus keep herself safe somehow.

She'd said she would still sleep with him but she wouldn't marry him. She didn't want to live in the palace as his wife forever. That was a hard no from her. And if he insisted? She would become disenchanted. She would become resentful. She would try to run away again. And he didn't think he could stand that.

He'd wanted to do right for the child but also do right for her. To give her as much freedom as he could allow. But there was no real compromise in this situation as it currently stood. There couldn't be. And now he liked her. He even cared about her. Which made it all the more imperative to stop this in its tracks now. He shouldn't have brought her back to the city. He shouldn't have shown her off in public. In doing so he'd put her more at risk than she'd already been. Now there was such speculation and a lot of it was accurate. But if he moved swiftly, decisively, then he could fix this.

He was the king. He could make a proclamation. He could recognise his child. Niko *needed* not just to listen to her but *hear* her.

He leaned against the wall. He really didn't feel good. A selfish part of him didn't want to relinquish his hold on her. But the lust still consuming him would surely fade.

She'd said all along that she wanted her freedom. He'd never realised or understood how and why she so deeply needed it. But she'd had virtually none. She'd had to work almost all of her life—without the recompense anyone should ordinarily get for it. She'd had no chance to explore and find out what she really wanted to do. She hadn't ever had her own choices.

She'd wanted to go shopping on her own and he'd been too selfish to even understand that. He'd wanted to see her joy—as if, what, he could feel *smug* about being the one to provide her with that experience? He'd made it all about him and never really considered her true wishes. He'd never really understood her—or what her motivations were. And she was still trying to accommodate him.

Of course he'd wanted her to have everything. He'd wanted to spoil her. He'd genuinely thought he'd tried. He thought he'd been understanding, patient and generous. He winced at his self-delusion. As if he could save her somehow?

But he knew better than most how one could live in the most beautiful place in the world, and have all the riches in the world. But those things didn't mean *happiness*.

And Maia had also had very little love. She'd had little time for fun and friendships and play. His head ached as he worked through the most unpalatable prospect that perhaps she'd only stepped into his bed *because* of that lack of affection. Perhaps it was exactly as those jerks had tried to do on her boat that time.

She liked him purely because he was one of the few people in her life who'd actually been nice to her. He'd made her *feel* good and she'd mistaken that for thinking that *he* was good. And he realised now he was *not* good enough for her. Because he'd wanted to put power and duty first—not a *person*. Which meant he was just like his grandfather after all. Overlooking someone's very existence in order to not disrupt the lineage. Niko had been prepared to overlook her unhappiness. He'd been so arrogant he'd assumed he could make her happy *enough*. But *that* wasn't good enough. And none of this was good for the stability of Piri-nu. He'd been making rash decisions that had only worsened the situation.

But now he knew exactly what he had to do.

'What's happened now?' Maia stared as Niko walked into the room, carefully closing the door behind him.

His unusual pallor instantly raised her concern. She'd never seen him pale.

'Has something else happened?' She swallowed. 'My father—'

'Has gone. It's not him.' He paced to the window.

She watched, her anxiety spiking as he seemed pull his thoughts together.

'I just wanted to clarify your...' He hesitated and cleared his throat. 'Proposal for how we might move forward from here.'

Her mouth dried. 'Oh?'

'You were saying that you're happy to continue being my lover, but that you won't marry me. Is that correct?'

She nodded, unsure about the rapid return to that awkward conversation and the even more awkward

way he was summing it up. He was like a robot all of
a sudden.

'How long did you think the intimate aspect of our
relationship would last?' he asked.

'I...' Now *she* had to clear her throat. 'As long as it
was convenient, I guess.'

He nodded thoughtfully. 'And we would remain ex-
clusive for as long as that was convenient too. Is that
what you were thinking?'

Her stomach churned. She didn't want to answer that.
She didn't want to *contemplate* it.

But Niko didn't give her long to answer anyway.
'What happens when one or other of us wants to change
the situation?'

Did he mean when he was tired of her?

'Then I would live somewhere else,' she said me-
chanically. 'Somewhere nearby. I mean, the palace is
huge...' She watched him warily. 'Or I could find a
small apartment in a building not too far away.'

'But what about work? What would you like to do?'

Honestly, Maia hadn't thought *any* of this through
and she didn't know. Why did all that need to be decided now? Couldn't they just stop the marriage pressure and figure other things out as they went along?
But there was an implacable set to his features and she
felt a qualm. He was still—*only*—fixated on duty. He
was only offering marriage because she was pregnant
and her father had forced him into moving on that even
more quickly. But he was wrong. Of course she wanted
what was best of this baby but they could achieve that—
better—without being married. Because she now felt a
strong, desperate need to ensure *she* too was safe. Last

night she'd realised the extent of her feelings and if she were to marry him, it would destroy her. Because he didn't feel the same.

'I don't know,' she admitted softly. 'I could always go back to the island.'

'But you enjoyed last night.' Inexorably he found fault with her suggestion. 'You wanted more in your life than what the island offers. You want to be able to shop or go to the theatre, the movies even, a sports game. All those things.'

'That doesn't matter,' she mumbled.

'What you want doesn't matter?' He looked at her intently. 'That's unacceptable to me, Maia.'

But what she *really* wanted was impossible. Unspeakable.

He folded his arms across his chest. Looking bigger, tougher. Closed off. 'You're going to Australia this afternoon.'

'What?'

'Australia. This afternoon. The tickets are just being arranged right now. We're expediting a passport for you.'

'What?' She couldn't have heard properly. She stared at him as the words sank in. He'd been gone so long and this was what he'd been doing? 'You're sending me away?'

'Yes.'

She stared at him, trying to work out why. Last night had been amazing. She'd felt on top of the world. But there was a catch because it wasn't actually *real*, was it? It was a pretence. A convenience. It meant nothing. And he'd had enough of her. Already. So quickly. The novelty of her had worn off and there was nothing left to interest him. Only she couldn't quite believe that all those moments had been that shallow. She couldn't believe that he felt *nothing*.

'Is this because I won't marry you?' She began to get angry. 'Are you so annoyed that I won't agree to *everything* you want that you're punishing me?' She stepped closer in disbelief. 'Are you that spoilt, Niko?'

'This is not a punishment.' He stared at her. 'That's the opposite of my intention. I want you to have your freedom, Maia.'

Her freedom? She stood very still as a horrible feeling opened up within her. 'Don't tell me you're doing this in my best interests…'

'But this is exactly what's best, Maia.'

'Not if I get no *choice*,' she argued.

'Well, you don't. Not immediately,' he said grimly. 'Initially I need to be sure you're safe. We have a home there that is already serviceable.'

Serviceable. 'And then? What's the long-term plan, Niko?'

'It's best if you go right away.' He didn't answer her actual question. 'I think it will be easier for you to adjust to the change in our relationship.'

She stared, bereft of speech as the horror of the situation grew. 'The…' Fear whispered out. 'You don't want me at all anymore?'

'It's not helping either of us,' he said grimly.

Helping? She couldn't even echo the madness.

Was it normal to have the best night of your life and then have it fall apart? How had she felt something so vastly different to him? How could they be so completely opposite in their assessment of that experience? Was she this naive? This inexperienced in relationships?

'I know you're upset,' he gritted. 'But—'

'Yes. I am. Shall we blame it on pregnancy hormones?' she interrupted, her mouth running off before her brain could stop it. 'Or say it's because I'm inexperienced? But they're both just excuses to dismiss my *feelings* because you're uncomfortable with the fact that you've just hurt me.' She blinked rapidly. 'Because you *have*, Niko.'

She hated that acidic tears were so close. She never cried. But even though she swallowed she couldn't stop the rising emotion. 'You broke your promise.'

'Which is why it's better to do this now before it gets worse.'

'*It?*' She stared at him, humiliated, and yet defiance surged. She would not apologise for having *feelings*. 'You mean how I *feel* about you?'

He glanced away. Apparently looking at her was now too awkward. 'You're confused, Maia.'

Oh, wow. Was he really going to dismiss what she felt and thought and experienced? Did he really think he 'knew better'?

'Then clarify this for me, Niko,' she invited coldly. 'Explain all. Why am I being sent away and how long for?'

'I think we need time and space apart. This is too much for you to have to make decisions on right now.'

She paused. So this was coming from a place of protectiveness? She narrowed her gaze. 'Why the sudden switch when less than an hour ago you were chomping at the bit to announce our engagement?'

'I've had a chance to think more clearly.'

He'd had time away from her. And he was worried about the decisions she'd tried to make—her determination that she would *not* marry him. That had truly bothered him—why? Did he want her to change her mind? Hope—almost destroyed—suddenly fluttered again.

She stood and walked towards him. 'Did last night mean anything for you?' she asked and took all her courage in her hands. 'Because it meant something to me, Niko. And I don't want to go away. I want to stay here with you. We can work this out—'

'No.' He stomped on that flicker of hope. 'This isn't right. It's asking too much of you, Maia.'

Why had he suddenly leapt to that conclusion?

'You think you're the only one capable of handling hard things? I'm just as strong as you. If not stronger.' She gazed at him, trying to understand what he was thinking. 'And I'm not your mother, Niko. I'm tough. I've survived so much more than you'll ever really know.'

'Yeah, and you shouldn't have to survive more. You should just have—' He broke off. 'Whatever you want.'

'Then why not *ask* me what I want instead of making some unilateral decision? Instead of assuming that you know everything? Why not listen to what I'm telling you. I want—'

'You *can't* know what you want!' he fired back in frustration. 'You've never had the chance to even understand all your options.'

She sucked in a breath. 'So no matter what I say, you won't believe that I might *want* to stay with you?'

'It's irrelevant because you *can't*.' He stared at her stonily. 'Because *I* don't want you to.'

And what he wanted happened.

'I only want what is best for you,' he said.

'You only want what's *easy*,' she shot back.

'You think this is easy?' he retorted furiously. 'It would be *much* easier to make you stay here with me, Maia, and you know *exactly* how I could get you to set aside your resistance.'

She stared at him, her heart shattering as he admitted using his skill to seduce her. To manipulate her. But she also knew he was wrong. 'But you can't, can you, Niko? You've realised you can't. You can seduce me to a mindless mess but I'll still say no to marriage. You know I won't change my mind. And you can't cope with that.'

They glared at each other.

'You're right. I don't want you forced into staying here.'

'But I do want to stay. I just don't want to marry you.'

'Why not? Why am I good enough to sleep with and not good enough to marry?' he asked.

His twist of reality all but destroyed her and the truth spilled out. 'Because this isn't going to last. Because you're not in love with me.'

He stared at her. 'You do not need me. You do not need *this*. Go, Maia. You be everything you want to be. Do it all. Discover everything. Please, I want that for you.'

Not *I want you*. But *I want that* for *you*.

She heard the nuance and understood. He really didn't want her.

'You've been fighting for your freedom for all this

time and now I want to help you get it and you're suddenly all angry with me?' He threw his hands up. 'I can't win.'

'Because everything's changed.' She stared at him pleadingly. 'Hasn't it?'

He shook his head. 'It's just been an intense few days.'

'No. That's not all.' She stared at him, willing him to admit even just a little to the truth of their connection.

'Don't, Maia.'

'Don't speak the truth?'

'You can't even know what that is,' he said heavily. 'You have no basis for comparison. You've been isolated your whole life. You haven't had the chance to find out what you might want. How can you really understand anything you think you feel?'

So he *was* using her inexperience against her. There was nothing she could say to convince him otherwise. Because he still wasn't listening to her. He wanted her *gone*.

Badly. Because he cared. But not enough about *her*. Not in the way of him actually wanting her. Not enough to try.

'I want you to be free to be who you are.'

'I am with you,' she said. 'I don't hold back with you. I'm not afraid of you. And I'm not afraid to ask for what I want with you.' And she couldn't be afraid now. 'It's just that I want more. Of you.' She drew a deep breath. 'I only want *you*, Niko. That's all.'

She wanted the best for him too.

He flinched. 'You're not staying here, Maia. Do you

understand? We're not ever getting married. I will never ask you again.'

She froze. 'But you said—'

'It doesn't matter what I said. I was wrong. It's not in your best interests.'

He was being so patronising. Furious, she glared at him. 'And the baby?'

'Will have my name. Will be my heir. But will be free to make their own choices when they're old enough.'

He wanted what *he* thought was best for her. Because in his way he did care. But not in the way she wanted. She wanted him to care so much that he'd be *unable* to let her go. She'd never been wanted just for herself and she still wasn't. She wanted him to hold her and keep her. Always. And it was *such* a stupid, impossible fantasy, but she couldn't get it out of her head. Because last night had been *so* amazing. 'And that's just it for us? We're over?'

He stiffened.

'Why won't you compromise?' she asked. 'Why isn't this enough?'

Couldn't they make this work just as it was?

'I'm sorry, Maia—'

'I don't want you to feel sorry for me,' she snapped, her voice raw with emotion. 'I want you to *love* me!'

He stared at her. Silenced.

'But you know what? I feel sorry for you. You can't be honest, can you? You can't admit anything deeply personal. You won't let yourself be vulnerable. Because you've been hurt.' His heart had been broken by his parents. 'All those women you dated? You said yourself they were safe choices. But that was because *you* never had to invest emotionally. You took what you wanted. Fun, frolics. A few laughs. Little more. Your *heart* was never at risk. You literally had nothing to lose. It was shallow and fun. But you could walk away at any time and you did. But you *can't* walk away from me, Niko.' She stared at him. 'And now you can't cope with me. So you're *sending* me away instead.'

'It's not that I can't cope with you.'

'No?' She rose and walked towards him. 'Isn't that exactly what this is?'

'I don't want you to be hurt. You've had enough pain.'

'We've all been hurt, Niko. Everyone gets scared. But you have to be brave to get the good things. They don't just come to you. They don't just happen.'

He shook his head at her.

'I know your mum struggled.' She looked him directly in the eye. 'And I know you feel things deeply. You're a highly sensitive person, Niko.'

He was frozen. Staring at her.

'So *you* don't take personal risks. You said you wanted to protect me. And this baby. But you're really only protecting yourself. This distance you want is like a shield.' She stared up at him. 'You don't want to have to be responsible for someone else's happiness. You don't have to do anything to make me or this baby happy. All you have to do is open up and let me in.'

She paused. Waiting. Hoping.

But he didn't answer.

CHAPTER THIRTEEN

'She's landed safely,' Pax informed Niko from the doorway.

Niko nodded, not looking up from the paperwork he'd been struggling to process for the last two hours. 'You have someone watching over her?'

'From a distance, yes. She was adamant she didn't want a minder.'

Niko gritted his teeth. He could just imagine her irritation but he was determined that she would be safe there in the Australian coastal city. She would be able to explore all she wanted, at least for a little, before the baby was born. She could have some freedom while he figured out a better future for her. Distance was the best course of action right now.

It would be hard not to have his child on the islands full-time, but this child needed their mother and Maia wanted to give them everything she'd not had. Niko would not stand in the way of that. He'd had the good fortune of having a mother's love and he wanted his child to know that too. Eventually he'd devise a visitation and an education plan so the child would understand its heritage…he would make this work.

He realised Pax was still standing in the doorway and he glanced up questioningly. Pax's expression was even more impassive than usual.

'What is it?' he asked, suddenly wary. 'Is something wrong?'

After a beat Pax stepped forward and closed the door behind him. 'There is a problem in Monrayne.'

'Monrayne?' Niko stood immediately. 'What is it? Pax?'

'I have to go.' Pax removed the sunglasses from his face, revealing the jagged scar above his left eyelid and his ice blue eyes. 'I realise this is unfortunate timing.'

'No, it isn't.' Niko dismissed Pax's apology and welcomed the rising concern. They'd been there for each other since boarding school and he would do anything he could for his friend. 'Everything is settled here now.'

Pax's gaze turned sardonic but Niko didn't want to talk about Maia anymore. This was exactly what he needed. Something to think of outside of himself. Only Niko knew the secret his security chief had hid for the last decade—Pax Williams wasn't only a soldier. Pax Williams wasn't even his name.

'You must go,' Niko said firmly. 'You must do what is right.'

Pax looked at him steadily. 'As must you.'

Niko stiffened and his resolve hardened. 'Yes. I'll go with you.'

'*No*.' The cloak of obedience fell away and Pax denied him imperiously. 'I'll handle this my way, Niko. You *do* have matters to attend to here,' he added with the implacable authority of the prince he really was.

'Perhaps it's not only about doing what is right, but also doing what you *want*.'

Niko didn't appreciate the unwanted advice. Besides, hadn't Niko been doing only what he *wanted* for years?

He shut down the conversation by bowing to his friend instead. 'If you need anything—'

'I know.' Pax nodded brusquely.

But Niko knew he wouldn't take up the offer because Captain Pax Williams was the long-lost Prince Lucian of the Central European kingdom of Monrayne. And if he was finally ready to reclaim his title, he now needed no one.

Niko stared at the door long after Pax had shut it behind him and desperately determined that he needed no one either.

Not *ever*.

In theory Maia could do anything she wanted. Go anywhere. See anything. She had money, a maid in the rooms next door. She had a driver and a car at her disposal 24/7. For the first time in her life, her time was completely her own. And she had no idea what to do with it.

She'd promised Niko's scary silent soldier friend that she would stay in the city, and she genuinely didn't want to cause any of them any more trouble.

She'd said Niko was a coward. He wasn't. He'd been braver than she had. It was mortifying but he'd been honest in refusing her offer of compromise. He wouldn't take advantage of her any longer. It was her own fault it had happened in the first place. She'd made it so easy for him. She'd launched herself into his bed within twenty-four hours of meeting him. So starved of attention she'd said yes in seconds. She'd behaved exactly how those horrible guests on the boat had once joked she would...

But oddly she couldn't regret it. It had been good. And if it were only a good time then maybe she'd be able to get over it swiftly.

But it hadn't only been a good time. It had been *him*. He'd made her *laugh*. He'd made her feel seen and heard. He'd made her feel strong and beautiful and special. And he was too easy to like—not just to *lust* after but actually like. He was sharp and kind, incisive, amusing, outrageous. And hurt. There was that deeply hurt side hidden in him too.

He'd wanted to do what he believed was right. So he wasn't all that selfish and spoilt really. He was dutiful and aware of the impact of his world upon others. But he didn't love her. For about five minutes there she'd thought she could have it all. But he didn't want that. Not with her.

Maia needed that. She needed a man who loved her. Someone who was honest and brave.

So she needed to figure out what to do with her new-found *time*. It wasn't enough to not have to worry about her money. She needed purpose and dignity and a passion for herself. That she could put everything into before the baby arrived. And then she would pour all her love into that sweet child.

And she would be okay. She would survive. She had no choice but to.

* * *

It was almost two weeks before Niko braved the island but in the end he had no choice. The hellish headache had been building for days. A migraine, he figured. His first. Some small semblance of the sort his mother had suffered. *Stress*.

In the end he took the helicopter. He'd stay just the one night. He'd relax and shake off the relentless throb in his temple. But as he stared moodily across the water and the house came into view he'd honestly never felt more miserable. It was self-indulgent and weak. He dropped his bag in the bedroom. He'd asked Aron to remove the hammocks before he arrived but he still saw them in his mind's eye. Every damned room was haunted by her presence.

He walked out to the pool and saw the small carving on the table Aron had set for one.

'Where did you find it?' he asked the elderly man when he wheeled a silver trolley out.

'It was tucked away in a little corner of her deck. I found it when I took down the hammock as you requested. I'm not sure if it was meant to be found.'

No, she'd have thought she'd stowed it safely. Leaving a little marker of herself hidden away.

He picked up the beautiful sea turtle and studied closely the intricate way she'd inlaid some small stones into its shell. The stones he'd found on the beach. The ones she'd won from him. She'd used a couple of obsidian chips for eyes. A tiny tormenting treasure to remind him not just of her, but of her skill. And her strength in adversity. She created beautiful things out of whatever little scraps she had to hand. So what would she build if she had more resources to play with? Something infinitely beautiful.

Something *priceless*.

He became aware that Aron was scrutinising him equally closely.

'I know what you're thinking,' Niko said.

'I'm sure you do—'

'Stop it. I already know I've screwed up.' He sighed heavily. 'Bring me a bottle of whisky, will you?'

'You might have another headache tomorrow, sir.'

Niko put the sea turtle down. 'I'm quite sure I will.'

But once Aron had fetched the bottle and then left him alone Niko simply stared at the amber liquid. The path of his father when he'd lost his wife. The devastation of losing the love of his life had led him into such poor choices—self-medicating his suffering. Only suffering more. Causing suffering too—to Niko. To Aron. To himself.

Niko would not do the same.

His family weren't fabulous at loving others healthily. His grandfather had failed to love his daughter, Lani. He'd failed to even *acknowledge* her.

He'd seen his father struggle to balance the expectations of his grandfather and the care his wife needed. And her accident had destroyed his father. But his mother had shown him the way forward, hadn't she? She'd striven to teach him balance in their time here. Making him stop to rest and recharge in nature. To count the stones, to fish and appreciate the ocean's bounty, to run in the sands where his ancestors had thrived for centuries.

But it had taken Maia to point that out to him. She had taken her sharp little knife and shaved away the pieces that he preferred to keep in place. She'd peeled away that protective layer with her challenge, her wit and her warmth. She'd left him exposed, revealing the truth of his loneliness. His hurt. His guilt. His fear.

And now he longed for the sweet balm of her body. He could bury himself in her and ignore the world. But that wasn't enough for her. She wanted—and deserved—more. So he'd sent her away. He'd thought he was so honourable. Putting her well-being first. Letting her be 'free.' 'Protecting' her.

But she was right about that too.

He'd been protecting *himself.* Hiding his heart. But she'd tried to fight for him. Only he'd been too blinded by fear to realise it.

But she didn't think good things could just happen for her. She thought she had to work for them somehow—had to put herself on the line, had to be willing to accept *less.*

Why won't you compromise?

Why isn't it enough?

He couldn't agree to her outrageous concubine offer because it had felt *wrong.* Only now did he realise just why.

She shouldn't have had to do that. She should have *everything.* The security and freedom to be found within love. She shouldn't have to *fight* for everything she wanted or needed. She should be given it. She never had though, had she? She'd never had the unconditional, unwavering love every person should have. She should always know just how deeply, how truly and how passionately she was loved. She should never doubt it. *Ever.*

He'd let her down so badly.

But she was strong, a survivor. She would be surviving just fine right now. *He* was the one who wasn't.

He was sensitive. He had been distracting himself with safe affairs. He'd been avoiding the decisions about his future not because he didn't want to hurt someone else, not because he didn't want the emotional responsibility for someone else, but because *he* didn't want to lose any more. *He* was hurt.

She'd thought he wanted her only because of the baby. That couldn't be more wrong. But he'd not been brave enough to be honest with her. But the truth was he'd not gotten his balance back from the moment he'd stepped on board that boat. She'd upended his world. Not the baby. But Maia herself. And baby or not, he wanted Maia. He missed Maia. He loved Maia.

And he wanted her back.

CHAPTER FOURTEEN

IT WAS A good thing Pax had gone to the other side of the world. He'd be apoplectic about the risk he'd consider Niko was currently taking. No bodyguard. Economy class as incognito as he could. Then public transport. He'd have driven himself to the apartment but he'd not slept at all on the flight and knew it would be dangerous to drive. But he got there and it was with a mix of terror and relief that he finally knocked on the door.

There was no answer. He knocked again. Waited. Then let himself in.

'Maia?' he called and checked every room with increasing desperation. He'd wanted to see her so badly and she wasn't here. In the end he sank onto the sofa in the lounge, setting the sea turtle on the small table in front of him. He'd wait. But he'd not slept the whole flight. He'd been planning everything he wanted to say—not daring to imagine her response—so desperate to see her, but he'd not imagined that she wouldn't be here. Now he didn't know where she was and it *sucked*. He pressed his hands to his eyes in a futile attempt to stop the stinging disappointment and sheer desolation.

'Niko?'

Oh great. Now he was hallucinating.

'What are you doing here?'

He dropped his hands and blinked. Yeah, he was definitely hallucinating, because Maia was right in front of him, clad in the gorgeous yellow bikini she'd worn the day he'd made love to her for the first time. He just groaned—helpless, wordless, devastated.

'What's wrong?' The apparition knelt down before him. 'Are you ill?'

He froze as a decidedly real, warm hand softly pressed against his cheek.

Shit. Was she really here? He grabbed her wrist and held her hand to him. 'Maia?'

She immediately stood—her arm now stretched out awkwardly. 'What's happened? Is it Aron? You look…'

'Terrible? I feel terrible.' He reluctantly released her wrist and shook his head. 'I didn't think you were here. I thought you'd gone.'

She looked at him warily. He didn't blame her.

'I was in the pool up on the roof,' she explained. 'What are you doing here?'

'I made a mistake. A big one.' He was suddenly trembling and his brain was doing a very bad job of remembering everything he'd wanted to say.

'You're not supposed to be here.' Maia was struggling to cope with the shock of finding him in the apartment. And he'd brought the small turtle she'd left on her balcony on the island. She'd hidden it there, a secret reminder that Maia was there—*once*—but he'd found it and brought it with him. Now she needed to move because she was about to lose all emotional control and she wasn't doing that in front of him again.

'Maia—'

'No.' She stepped back from him. 'No.'

He suddenly stood, suddenly huge and overpowering, and her barely taped together heart shattered.

'Maia, darling. Please—'

'No.' This time her denial wasn't for him, but for herself. She was desperate to stop the tears—to stop him seeing. She tried to run but he drew her against him before she could—wrapping his arms right around her so tightly like the morning he'd first met her.

'Maia.' He whispered her name in her hair as he cradled her in such a strong, secure embrace. Holding her so safe that every emotion tore free.

'Please don't do this to me,' she pleaded into his solid frame. 'I can't go through this again. I can't—'

'I'm sorry.' He pressed her closer into his chest, stroking her back, clearly feeling her whole body trembling. 'I'm sorry I didn't tell you everything. I couldn't admit it. But now I'm here and—'

'*Why?*' she cried angrily, pushing back enough to look up at him. 'Why are you here? What do you want?'

'I want…' He drifted off, staring into her eyes for such a long time and heaven help her, Maia just fell for him all over again—lost in the gleaming intensity of his warm brown gaze. Something new flowed through her—settling her pulse, slowing her breathing—*certainty*.

'Wondered if you'd do dinner,' he finally mumbled.

'Maybe a movie. Get married. Make love. Lots. Have this baby. Live a long time. Love each other always. That was pretty much the plan. Figured other details might…might…' He suddenly sighed, a shuddering release of yearning.

She blinked and tears spilled.

'Maia.' He wiped her cheeks gently and rested his forehead on hers, his eyes gleaming with the thing she'd never dared dream of seeing. 'I don't want to compromise. I don't want "just enough." In this I am spoilt. I am selfish. I want *everything* possible.' He drew breath. 'But most of all I want *you* not to have to compromise. *You* should have everything. I just hope that you still might want to have *me*.'

She couldn't move. It was like it had been from the beginning. He stole her breath, made her brain dizzy, made her body melt.

'I'm not asking because I feel like I have to, ought to, should…' he breathed. 'I'm asking only because I want to. So badly. Because I'm so bloody miserable without you, Maia.'

All she could do was lean in close and it was enough. The kiss ignited everything. She clutched him.

'Missed you,' he muttered again and again between kisses. 'Don't go away ever again.'

'Don't *send* me away ever again.'

'Yeah. Never.' His beautiful smile was filled with apology. 'Oh.' He suddenly stiffened. 'I found Stefan.'

'What?'

'I tracked Stefan down. He's spent the last few years

moving from job to job. He was glad to hear you're well and that you've left your father's boat.'

'Why did you go looking for him?'

'Because he was nice to you and he was badly treated by your father. Which is the absolute opposite of what should have happened. I wanted to see if he was okay or if he needed anything.'

Niko's thoughtfulness, kindness and honour awed her. 'And did he?'

'I offered him a part-time retirement job on the island. Aron can only make salads and I thought that our children might like a sweet pastry with breakfast.'

'Our *children*?'

'I half hoped you might want more than one? I'd like a big loving family.' He hesitated, his eyes widening. 'But only if you do too. When you do. I mean you haven't had much choice around—'

She put her hand on his mouth. 'I would love a big loving family. Thank you for finding him for me. For even thinking of it.'

The bikini was gone in moments. His shirt and trousers were slightly more troublesome but they got there.

'I've never had someone want me,' she whispered. 'Someone really and truly just want *me*.'

'*I* do. So completely.' He braced above her. 'And I offer you all of *me*.' He tightened his hold. 'My arms to hold you. My ears to listen to anything you want to tell me or even just to tease me. My whole body really, however you want me.'

'Now, I want you now.' She'd missed him so much

she was already hot and ready and they both groaned as he pushed home.

'I offer my loyalty. My fidelity. I'll only ever be yours, Maia. Because you have my heart. I didn't want to admit that before because I was scared and I'm sorry about that. But I love you, Maia. And I'm here and I don't ever want to let you go again.'

He thrust deep, pressing closer and closer still—anchoring her to him. She wrapped around him and simply hung on. Letting him love her. Letting him take her so fast, so intensely, she couldn't even scream. She simply shook—and he just held her closer still, until he groaned with agonising ecstasy.

Maia couldn't move after that cataclysmic release. She felt as if she'd been tossed through every emotion and was utterly wrung out. All that remained was joy.

She lifted her head just enough to catch his eye and smiled. 'Is that all you've got?'

He began to laugh and she too giggled. But suddenly her laughter turned to tears and he swiftly wrapped his arms around her again—so tightly.

'I've got you,' he muttered.

She knew the reassurance was not just for her, but for him too. She hugged him tightly back and as her sobs eased she heard his sigh of aching contentment.

Her longing. Her absolute truth escaped her too. 'I love you, Niko.'

'Thank you,' he whispered.

His fingers rhythmically combed through her hair in a tender touch of love. Of wonder. She closed her eyes. Jewels and thrones and things meant little—what she'd found with him was family and yes, *freedom*. To be herself, to ask for what she wanted—to give and to take. Because there was no freedom more complete than that she'd found in the security of his love.

CHAPTER FIFTEEN

Almost three years later

PRINCESS KAILANI LIKED to splash her father. Repeatedly. King Niko sat in the shallow end of the pool and patiently helped his toddler refill the little bucket—that she would then tip all over him. And giggle. And immediately refill it again.

Niko didn't mind. He loved his daughter, the sunshine, the *time* that he had to do this.

'Mama?' Kailani questioned, staring at him with her big brown eyes.

'Soon. She'll be home soon,' he answered, distracting her with a different water toy.

Honestly, he couldn't wait for Maia to arrive either. She'd had a meeting on a nearby island and frankly he'd expected her to be here already. He'd seen some coverage on his tablet earlier—Maia sitting in a circle of dignitaries discussing ship workers' rights. Sometimes he was so filled with awe of her he didn't know what to do with himself. She'd flourished, his beautiful wife. Popular with his people, down to earth, she had an accessibility and relatability that other royals from nearby nations had told him they wished they could bottle. He got it—she had a quality, a resilience and a generosity, that was rare and that he would never ever take for granted. Often they worked together but sometimes for practical reasons they took on separate engagements. That was what had happened today. But Niko's straightforward plaque unveiling had concluded sooner than anticipated so he'd been able to bring Kailani to the island a little earlier than planned. While Maia's meeting had run late.

Aron shuffled out from where he'd been sitting in the shade. 'The boat is almost here.'

Niko had thought the old man had been dozing—apparently not. Apparently he too was watching for Maia. 'Great.'

'I've just taken the pain au chocolat from the oven.' Stefan appeared in the doorway, looking pleased with the timing.

Yeah, Niko and Kailani definitely weren't the only ones watching for the return of their queen.

Niko lifted his daughter into his arms and carried her down the beach to the water's edge to greet her. It was a glorious day—above and before them the blue expanse stretched to infinity. There was no storm coming, only heat. He could see her sitting in the stern, her glorious long black hair gleaming in the late afternoon sun. Her smile flashed as she watched him encourage their daughter to wave at her.

She waved back and there was such a sparkle in her eyes Niko melted. The entire weekend stretched before them. They scheduled at least two whole weekends here each month to have completely to themselves. It was part of the balance they'd carefully worked to achieve together. Barefoot, Maia jumped into the water, not caring that the hem of her pretty dress was soaked even though she'd hitched it up.

'I'm devastated you're wearing a swimsuit,' she whispered to him tartly, her smoky gaze drinking in his still-damp skin.

'Couldn't scare the staff. Or our daughter—you teasing wretch.' But Niko could kiss her—passionately—loving the equally hot, hungry welcome of her mouth.

Then he laughed as their child wriggled restlessly on his hip and held out her arms to her mama.

'I missed you,' he muttered as he lifted their daughter into Maia's embrace.

'It's been eight hours.' She kissed Kailani's sweet cheek.

'Yeah, and I missed you for all of them.'

She wrinkled her nose. 'Crazy man.'

'Crazy in love.' He slung his arm around her shoulders and drew her close and turned towards their beach home. His happiness right this second simply couldn't be surpassed.

But Maia glanced behind her shoulder and called back, 'Are you guys okay? Do you need help?'

'We're fine, thank you, ma'am.'

Niko had been so busy feasting his eyes on his wife he hadn't even noticed other people disembarking. Now he frowned. He didn't want *work* following them here. That wasn't the plan for this weekend at all.

'What's going on?' he asked Maia.

'I'm pre-empting your over-protectiveness.' Maia smiled at him impishly.

'My what?'

There was an odd light in her eyes now—a sheen that made him stop still right where he was, halfway up the beach with his feet bare and sandy. His plump toddler babbled sweetly, oblivious to the sudden tension filling her father.

'I'm ensuring you'll have all the reassurance *you* need,' she said.

Reassurance? For what? He turned and stared more closely at the cluster of people lifting boxes from the rear of the boat. He recognised one of the men. It was the doctor who'd cared for Maia when she was pregnant with Kailani. So he was here now because...?

Anticipation swept through him like a king tide. 'Maia,' he murmured throatily.

His wife simply smiled even more impishly.

He didn't need to be a rocket scientist to figure this one out. But at the same time it was so *good* he really didn't want to be wrong. He tugged her closer so he could whisper, 'Have you something to tell me?'

She giggled. He loved it when she giggled. When she teased him. When she looked at him like this—with love in her eyes and vitality oozing from every pore. He just gazed back at her. She'd never looked more beautiful.

And now his chest was so tight he couldn't breathe. 'You've already done a test?'

'Just this morning. Then I rang the doctor and asked him to come here.' She nodded. 'He's brought his fancy portable scanning machine with him,' she said. 'I didn't want to confirm it—or see anything—without you and

I also knew you wouldn't want to wait. You'll want all the information, immediately.'

Yeah, she was very right about that. But still he was stunned. 'We've only been trying a short—'

'And isn't that just typical of your...*stuff*?' she interrupted him with a laughing look.

He chuckled and pleasure flooded him. 'Stefan's been baking all afternoon in readiness for your arrival. I'm sure Kailani would enjoy a petite pastry with him and Aron while we meet with the specialist?'

Maia nodded. 'I've asked the maid to show him to our private lounge.'

Niko's tension proliferated. He needed to know. Now. Most especially that everything was okay—that *Maia* was okay.

Maia had known Niko would be impatient. Frankly she was too. It had almost been impossible to focus on her meeting today so she'd had to work extra hard and then she'd gotten fully into it and it had actually made time fly all the more quickly.

She set Kailani into her small chair and smiled as Aron and Stefan immediately fussed around the small girl. She rarely heard from her father and while that sometimes saddened her, there was so much more *to* be grateful for. Kailani had two grandfather figures who adored her and taught her so much. Maia too had their love and support. As did Niko.

After a few minutes she took her husband's hand and walked to the small lounge.

The doctor had set up his equipment. Maia smiled to herself as Niko paced about the room while the doctor

helped her. She'd never forget the sight of him standing at the beach clad in just his black swim shorts,
his bronze skin burnished in the sun, his tattoos drawing her gaze to his rippling muscles, his protective yet
playful hold of their child, his smile as he watched her
approach. He was stunning and that he was hers still
amazed her.

'This is earlier in the pregnancy and we need to do a
different scan from the first one we did when you were
pregnant with Princess Kailani,' the doctor explained.
'So don't worry that you're going to see less on the
screen.' He smiled apologetically at her. 'And unfortunately, it might be a little uncomfortable.'

Niko paced about even more quickly.

'It's okay,' Maia reassured him.

'I'm here for *you*,' he declared. 'You don't need to
worry about me.'

'But I can see *you* worrying.' She chuckled.

The scan was a little uncomfortable and seemed to
take much longer than the first one. Niko stopped pacing completely and just stood nearby, alternately staring
at her, then the screen, then her again while the doctor
just focused on the screen.

'Is everything okay?' Niko finally asked through
gritted teeth.

'Yes…' the doctor answered slowly. 'But—'

'But what?'

The doctor breathed out. 'There's more than one ges-
tational sac.'

Maia met her husband's startled look.

'Pardon?' Niko muttered hoarsely.

'There are two…' The doctor paused thoughtfully

again, his focus still intently fixed on the monitor. 'I'm just checking… Yes. Just the two that I can detect at this stage.'

Just the *two*? And what did he mean by 'at this stage'?

'You mean twins?' Niko clarified urgently. 'You mean we're having twins.'

The doctor finally smiled. 'Yes. Congratulations.'

Maia couldn't believe what she was hearing.

'It's very early and while it's not probable, it's also not impossible that there might be more,' the doctor explained. 'Sometimes little babies like to hide behind their siblings. But there are at least two in there—looking very good.' He glanced at Maia reassuringly. 'Looking just as they should.'

'Not impossible…' Niko echoed. Then he suddenly looked tense. 'Twins. Maybe triplets? Does this make everything more risky for Maia?'

'Of course we'll monitor Queen Maia very carefully all the way through this pregnancy. But she's very healthy and I see no reason why this won't progress perfectly normally.'

Niko puffed out a harsh breath. 'You'll stay within reach of us at *all* times.'

'Of course, Your Highness.'

'Thank you, Doctor.' Maia smiled and spoke more gently. 'You took such great care of me last time and Kailani and I were both fine. I know this will be fine too.'

The doctor flushed slightly. 'Thank you, ma'am.'

'Yeah, thanks…' Niko ruffled his hair, looking shell-shocked. 'Uh, would you mind…'

'Giving you privacy?' Beaming, the doctor bowed and swiftly left the room, closing the door behind him.

Niko dropped to his knees beside her. 'Maia—'

'You have a real talent for over-achieving,' she said dazedly.

His smile was shamelessly smug for a second but then it faded and emotion welled in his eyes. 'No, I'm just unbelievably lucky,' he muttered huskily. 'I've never been more grateful in my life for that screw-up at the clinic that day. The thought of never meeting you otherwise?' He cupped her face in his hands. 'Of you being stuck on that bloody boat? Of us not having all of this together? I can't bear to think about it.'

'I know.' Tears spilled. It was silly because she'd never been as happy and here she was crying. 'Hormones already.' She wiped her cheeks inelegantly. 'Zillions of them, apparently.'

With a laugh he kissed her and she clung to him with desperate need. They had such riches already and such joy to come. The big family they both wanted would be here even quicker than they'd planned and she was so excited.

'Oh.' She pressed her hand to her forehead. 'I'm hot and flustered. I need a shower.'

'Happily, I have the best shower in the world.' He stood and scooped her into his arms.

'I'm still capable of walking,' she teased even as she clung to him delightedly.

'Indulge me in my primeval need to demonstrate my strength and ability to care for my woman,' he growled.

'Oh,' she breathed meekly. 'Okay then.'

And care for her he did. In the lush outdoor shower

where thick tropical foliage screened them, he removed her pretty dress with such gentleness and such tease it was a good thing he was there to help her remain standing.

'You were amazing today. Your speech was fantastic.' He carefully soaped, then rinsed, then kissed every inch of her body.

'You watched it?' She sighed dreamily.

'Of course I did.' He scooped her up again and carried her back inside to their bed.

'Twins,' Maia marvelled in wonder as he placed her onto the cool linen. 'Isn't it a good thing we live in a palace with an abundance of bedrooms.'

'You know they'll be banging our door down early in the morning to come crawl into bed with us. Kailani already does that.' Laughter and heat danced in his eyes.

'Then isn't it a good thing we have a big bed.'

'Think we better make the most of it now, actually.' His gaze turned serious. 'I need to love you…'

'*Finally!*' She rubbed against him. 'Come on then…'

His smile returned. 'Those hormones driving you again, huh?'

'No.' She shook her head. She was all seriousness now. 'It's love.'

His kisses were hot, his touches tender as he gently slid down her body and tormented her with such intimate strokes of his tongue. Maia arched and trembled in his hold. She loved it when he gifted her orgasms like this. But she was greedy. She wanted more. She wanted it all.

But Niko paused. 'Are you sure you're okay for—'

'Indulge *me* in *my* primeval need…' she ordered him

in a passionate whisper. 'I'm so excited I need...' She wrapped her legs around his waist and pulled him to her in a wild challenge. '*This* is where I need all of your strength. This is where I need all of *you.*'

And she desperately, *desperately* needed him now.

'I didn't think I could feel any happier than I did standing by the water with Kailani watching you come home to us,' Niko said huskily, holding a mere inch above her—so still, so close, so hot. 'But this is just incredible.'

'*Yes!*'

There was no living through this moment without their full surrender to passion. He was everything— sweetly relentless, fiercely demanding. Maia sighed with desperate delight, meeting him with an animal fervour of her own as they pushed to the brink and beyond. She shattered as the exquisite sensations claimed her reason. She loved him as he loved her—with everything she had—*hard*. And then it was so soft, so complete, so intimate...and she was indescribably happy.

Eventually he summoned the strength to roll to his side. He smiled at her, his brown eyes brimming with joy. 'Let's go find Kailani. We need to tell her she's going to be a big sister. What do you think she's going to say? Lord, what are Aron and Stefan going to say?'

Maia giggled at his excitement. She felt it too. And she too felt such gratitude. Their gorgeous daughter was going to have *everything* they longed for her to have— as were their precious babies who'd yet to arrive—parents who were there for them, elders who adored them, a more balanced public life, siblings, security...

And love. Always there would be so much love.

* * * * *

If Impossible Heir for the King *left you wanting more, make sure to look out for the next instalment in the* Innocent Royal Runaways *duet coming soon!*

In the meantime, why not explore these other stories by Natalie Anderson?

Nine Months to Claim Her
Revealing Her Nine-Month Secret
The Night the King Claimed Her
Carrying Her Boss's Christmas Baby
The Boss's Stolen Bride

Available now!

#4129 INNOCENT'S WEDDING DAY WITH THE ITALIAN
by Michelle Smart

Discovering that her billionaire fiancé, Enzo, will receive her inheritance if they wed, Rebecca leaves him at the altar and gives him twenty-four hours to explain himself. He vows his feelings are real, but dare Rebecca believe him and succumb to a passionate wedding night?

#4130 THE HOUSEKEEPER'S ONE-NIGHT BABY
by Sharon Kendrick

Letting someone close goes against Niccolò Macario's every instinct. When he receives news that shy housekeeper Lizzie Bailey, the woman he spent one scorching night with, is pregnant, Niccolò is floored—because his only thought is to find her and claim his child!

#4131 BACK TO CLAIM HIS CROWN
Innocent Royal Runaways
by Natalie Anderson

When Crown Prince Lucian returns from the dead to reclaim his throne, he stops his usurper's wedding, creating a media frenzy! He's honor-bound to provide jilted Princess Zara with shelter, and the chemistry between the ruthless royal and the virgin princess sparks an urgent, irresistible desire...

#4132 THE DESERT KING'S KIDNAPPED VIRGIN
Innocent Stolen Brides
by Caitlin Crews

When Hope Cartwright is kidnapped from her convenient wedding, she's sure she should feel outraged. But whisked away by Cyrus Ashkan, the sheikh she's been promised to from birth, Hope feels something *far* more dangerous—desire.

HPCNMRA0723

#4133 A SON HIDDEN FROM THE SICILIAN
by Lorraine Hall
Wary of billionaire Lorenzo Parisi's notorious reputation, Brianna Andersen vowed to protect her baby by keeping him a secret. Now the Sicilian knows the truth, and he's determined to be a father! As their blazing chemistry reignites, Brianna must admit the real risk may be to her heart...

#4134 HER FORBIDDEN AWAKENING IN GREECE
The Secret Twin Sisters
by Kim Lawrence
Nanny Rose Hill is surprised when irresistible CEO Zac Adamos personally proposes a job for her in Greece looking after his godson! She can't let herself get too close, but can the innocent really walk away without exploring the unforeseen passion Zac has awakened inside her?

#4135 THEIR DIAMOND RING RUSE
by Bella Mason
Self-made billionaire Julian Ford needs to secure funding from a group of traditional investors. His solution: an engagement to an heiress, and Lily Barnes-Shah fits the bill perfectly! Until their mutual chemistry makes Julian crave something outside the bounds of their temporary agreement...

#4136 HER CONVENIENT VOW TO THE BILLIONAIRE
by Jane Holland
When Sabrina Templeton returns to the orphanage from her childhood to stop her former sweetheart from tearing it down, playboy CEO Rafael Romano offers a shocking compromise... He'll hand it over if Sabrina becomes his convenient bride!

HARLEQUIN
PLUS

Try the best multimedia subscription service for romance readers like you!

Read, Watch and Play.

Experience the easiest way to get the romance content you crave.

Start your **FREE TRIAL** at
<u>www.harlequinplus.com/freetrial</u>.